*Kristen Allen was looking forward to time away from painful memories.*

As Kristin made her way from the pavilion her footsteps clacked along the sidewalk. She walked through the darkness from one dim carriage lamp to another, and was not sure how far she'd gone before she realized that she was not alone.

Someone was walking behind her, rapidly gaining!

She started to turn off the sidewalk to the path that led to the cluster of rooms where she and Mandy were housed, when a steel strong grip contained in a smooth leather riding glove snaked out, encircled her wrist, and yanked her back.

Kristin felt her knees grow weak and buckle, then a tall, lean, very strong, and very angry cowboy jerked her upright, lifting her face to within inches of his.

Kristin gasped, then tried to scream, but she was unable to even speak or make any sound. Her eyes widened with fright and she searched the dark for a clue to her attacker's identity.

He gave a cold smile that was followed by a bitter, cutting laugh. And his eyes that had been so turquoise on the airplane became like blue-white lightning flashing to cleave a thunderous summer sky.

"Had to return again, huh?" he drawled mockingly. "Just couldn't stay away?

"Please—" Kristin whispered, swallowing hard, as her throat was dry and tight with tension and she felt a heartbeat away from bursting into tears. "There's some kind of mistake—"

**BRENDA BANCROFT** is a pen name of inspirational romance author Susan Feldake. At home in central Illinois with her husband, Steven, and four children she is employed as a writing instructor for a college-accredited correspondence school. In her spare time, she likes to hike, listen to country and western music, and fellowship with close friends.

**Books by Brenda Bancroft**

HEARTSONG PRESENTS
HP22—Indy Girl
HP30—A Love Meant to Be
HP35—When Comes the Dawn
HP62—A Real and Precious Thing

ROMANCE READER—TWO BOOKS IN ONE
(Under the pen name Susan Feldake)

RR7—For Love Alone & Love's Sweet Promise

Don't miss out on any of our super romances. Write to us at the following address for information on our newest releases and club information.

Heartsong Presents Readers' Service
P.O. Box 719
Uhrichsville, OH 44683

# There's Always Tomorrow

*Brenda Bancroft*

*Heartsong Presents*

**A note from the Author:**

*I love to hear from my readers! You may write to me at the following address:*

Brenda Bancroft
Author Relations
P.O. Box 719
Uhrichsville, OH 44683

ISBN 1-55748-706-5

**THERE'S ALWAYS TOMORROW**

*one*

Kristin Allen cocked her head and decided that she *had* heard the telephone shrill. She nudged her vacuum sweeper with the scuffed toe of her Reebok, threw down the shiny metal wand, and rushed to answer.

Cloth diapers, not always so easy to find because of the popularity of disposable brands, were the best cleaning rags as far as Kristin was concerned. And as the guiding force behind her own successful cleaning business, she was in a position to know.

Some months earlier when Kristin had gone into the local Southern Illinois department store and bought four dozen old-fashioned diapers, the smiling sales clerk had trilled such a congratulatory remark that Kristin hadn't the heart to disappoint the woman by admitting that polishing windows and dusting woodwork were probably the closest she'd ever personally come to finding a practical application for diapers. . . .

"Good afternoon, Ms. Allen!" Her caller broke in on her thoughts. "This is Sam Sherman down at the Tip Top Pet Supply and Feed Store here in Camden Corners."

Kristin sighed and frowned at her reflection in the mirror. The call was starting off with all the earmarks of a sales pitch.

"I have no pets," Kristin said quietly, as she prepared to give the man a polite brush-off and idly wondered since when had such specialty stores phoned around town to solicit business?

Mr. Sherman proceeded with what he had to say and Kristin was too startled at finding him on the line to bother to stop him. Her mind was scrambling with facts to the point where she scarcely heard the man's monologue.

Kristin's dark brow drooped into a suspicious frown. She glanced at herself in the spotless mirror, the telephone receiver crushed to her right ear, and her dust rag clenched in her left hand as a sudden thought nettled her.

That afternoon her black, curly, shoulder length hair was hidden beneath a faded red bandanna. Her face was devoid of makeup because it was her day off—when she cleaned the large Victorian home she rented with an option to buy—and she didn't have to fix herself up in order to feel presentable enough to go out in the world and face the public.

As the jovial feed store owner rattled on, taking the long way around to get to the point of his call, suddenly Kristin's indigo eyes flashed with annoyance when it occurred to her that he—a stranger—had reached her at her *unlisted* number!

Since moving to Camden Corners the year before she'd literally kept a log of all who possessed her private, unlisted telephone number. It was an odd arrangement for a cleaning woman to have a number that didn't appear in directory listings, she knew, but idiosyncrasies were tolerated in small towns. Her Roving Maid advertisement had provided only her post office box number, contained a request for interested parties to contact her with their numbers, and she'd promised that she would be in touch.

In New York City where she'd lived before coming to Camden Corners, half a nation away, she could've protected herself by retaining an answering service, something unavailable in the small rural area she now considered home.

Those she'd agreed to take on as clients, she did eventually provide with her home number, but she'd almost made them swear upon a Bible that they wouldn't give it out to a soul.

Just as Kristin's mind was progressing through the roll call of people privy to her number, and she was trying to figure out who was the guilty party, as she was starting to feel the sting of betrayal, she remembered that an unlisted number didn't prevent calls from those telemarketers who dialed consecutive numbers in order to catch the listed and unlisted alike.

But when she recalled that the owner of the Tip Top Pet

Supply and Feed Store had addressed her by name, a chill washed through Kristin. She felt the old, familiar sense of vulnerability flood over her, leaving her feeling weak and frightened in its wake.

"On behalf of the fine folks who produce Happy Trails Horse Feed, and our local dealership, Ms. Allen, I'd like to offer you sincere congratulations," Mr. Sherman said in an expansive tone.

"What is this? Some kind of joke?" Kristi interrupted in a voice just this side of hostile, but didn't wait for an answer. "If so, it's not funny. I'm a busy person, now if you'll excuse me. . ."

Kristi's words choked off and she felt tears burn in her eyes. Irrationally, she struggled to maintain composure. She hated that she still suffered moments of panic over the silliest, simplest things despite what time had passed since her entire sense of security had been shattered, leaving her feeling helpless and unprotected in a brutal and violent society.

"Oh, it's no joke, Ma'am," said the conciliatory gentleman on the other end of the telephone line. "You, Ms. Kristin Allen, are the Grand Prize Winner in the nationwide Happy Trails Horse Feed Sweepstakes contest! You and a companion will get to spend two glorious weeks at the Circle K Dude Ranch, a dream vacation site not far from Rapid City, South Dakota. In addition, you'll receive a check for five thousand dollars— which, I may point out—ain't hay!"

The feed store owner guffawed over his little joke, enjoying it sufficiently for the both of them, Kristin thought. From his manner she almost dared to believe him, then her logical nature came to the fore.

"Bu-but I didn't enter any contests," Kristi persisted. "I haven't been near a horse in years. I've never heard of Happy Trails Horse Feed. There must be a mistake."

"The sweepstakes staff is very careful, doing everything according to regulations, Ma'am. As the owner of the dealership listed on the entry stub, I just got the call with the pertinent information. They felt that I'd like to be the one to convey the good news to a local customer."

Kristin swallowed hard, realizing how ungrateful and obstinate she must sound.

"I've never patronized your business, Mr. uh. . .Sherman. It's not that I don't think the prizes are nice, they sound lovely indeed, but I don't feel that I deserve. . ."

"Maybe you didn't enter," Mr. Sherman broke in. "But obviously someone slipped a stub or two bearing your name into the box on the countertop by the cash register in my store. People do that all the time when there's a drawing. It's a neat way to surprise a friend with something really wonderful."

"But who?" Kristin asked, frowning, looking around her as if somewhere she'd locate a clue.

Mr. Sherman's voice was hearty. "It doesn't really matter who, although I'm sure you'll find out all in good time. Meanwhile, just enjoy the fact that you're our Grand Prize Winner. There will be documents from the corporate headquarters arriving by certified mail, and once they're signed, notarized, and returned to the proper officials, we can begin processing the release of your sweepstakes prizes. Have you anything to say? Something we can quote on the radio station and for the weekly newspaper?"

"I-I'm overwhelmed. Shocked. And. . .and. . ."

"Very happy?" the feed store owner prompted.

"Okay," Kristin agreed, the smile on her face reflecting the irony she experienced that made her feel oddly dismal, "very, very happy."

"Got it! Super!" the man cheerfully said, and she thought she heard the lead tip of his pencil snap off as he underlined the quote on a pad of paper. "There'll probably be someone from the local newspaper who'll want to take a picture of us presenting the check to you, Ms. Allen. This is big news in an area like this. It'll likely make the front page of the *Camden Corners Gazette*. It might even be good for two news items if you have a picture of yourself we could have so they can run one announcing you as the winner in this week's edition, and another candid photograph when you accept your check. . ."

"A front page picture? Wow. . . ." Kristin said and her pulse galloped with a horrible sense of trepidation that sent her adrenaline levels soaring.

And what a comedown, Kris thought, as the silence spiraled, to go from teenage magazine cover girl to small town front page news item in two short years.

At the thought Kristin's mind froze. She was spiraled back in time, and suddenly she felt as if she were drowning in nightmarish memories and about to have her most closely guarded secrets held up for public scrutiny and gossipy speculation in an area she'd come to like and regard as home.

"No!" she said, and her voice was a thin gasp. "*No pictures!*" She clarified, trying to control her tone, hoping that the man from the feed store didn't correctly interpret her reaction for the raw terror it was. "I'm sorry. No," she repeated in what could almost be considered a normal tone.

"Gee. . .no picture we can use? What luck. . . . Oh well."

After covering a few more details the man ended the surprise call and Kristin was left with her thoughts.

Pictures? Did she have pictures? He wanted to know. Yes! Portfolios and albums full of them, interred in a coffin-like trunk she could no longer bear to open.

When Kristin was sixtenn her parents had been killed when their plane to Hawaii crashed on takeoff in Chicago. Her Aunt Delilah had taken custody of Kristin and her sister, Janice, and moved them to her New York City, Park Avenue apartment.

It was a life unlike either of the small town girls had experienced. With an important job at the U.N. Delilah traveled and socialized a great deal, so the girls were left alone a lot.

That arrangement was all right with Janice, a flirtatious, outgoing girl who was content to date almost every night, breaking a different heart each month. Jan and Aunt Dee were so busy with their own circumstances, and so alike, that they didn't seem to notice that Kristin was a lonely and introverted girl.

She studied hard, kept the apartment immaculate, read teen romance novels, mysteries, and adventure stories, bought all of the latest teen and fashion magazines, and for hours on end fussed with her hair and makeup while she dreamed of some-day having a true love of her own.

Some of Jan's old cast-off boyfriends eventually noticed Kristin and asked her out, but it became her habit to turn them down because she had a feeling that they felt as if they were settling for second best in her. Or even worse that they were trying to get even with her fickle big sister. Or even worse than *that*, that the boys were asking her out so they could remain nearby in the slim hope that Janice might relent and focus her attention on them again.

Then one day Kristin saw the Beauty Search details in one of her teen magazines. Even though her face was drenched almost fuschia with embarrassment, and she steeled herself against Janice making fun of her, she got up her courage and begged her big sister to donate an afternoon of her time to taking close-up color, instant pictures of her.

Janice's grudging attitude hadn't been good.

But the pictures of Kristin, when developed, were great.

Aunt Dee and Janice had exchanged amused smiles when Kristin had sent them off. She suspected that they'd shared whispered assessments that Jan was the true beauty in the family and that although Kristin looked remarkably like her older sister, she lacked the worldly veneer of sophistication that marked Jan's exceptional good looks. Instead, Kristin possessed an innocent patina on her features.

But they were no longer laughing when Kristi, selected as a finalist, was one of the lucky girls to be photographed by a professional, and eventually was the judge's final choice.

Kristin was groomed, instructed, made over, made up, coiffed, and presented on the front cover of her favorite teen magazine three months later. It was as if she'd been swallowed up by a whirlwind, for after that her life never seemed the same.

To her surprise, within a week Andre D'Arcy, head of a small but exclusive modeling agency, had contacted her, offering her a contract. His promises were enough to turn any young girl's head, and Aunt Dee warned her about dreaming of pie-in-the-sky. But obedient, hardworking, and pleasant, Kristin did everything Andre required, and as a result of her work and dedication, her one-time fantasies became thrilling reality as almost overnight she was in high demand as a teen-age model, commanding incredible hourly fees.

Kristin hadn't paid heed to Aunt Dee—or a snickering Janice—about spending so much time with Andre, an older man who obviously didn't return her feelings. She became unaware she existed outside the professional realm, and her social life became almost non-existent. As her face began to appear in so many ads and on various magazine covers, the few boys she knew who were near her own age acted like they wouldn't dare ask her out, so many nights she remained home alone and lonely.

Fortunately, Kristin now realized, she *had* listened when Aunt Delilah had pragmatically pointed out that Kristin's era of fame might not last. After all, Aunt Dee said, as she got older she might grow out of the teen model category and be unable to make the transition to the world of adult high fashion modeling. She could find herself out of work and untrained to be anything but a pretty face.

An astute woman, Dee had insisted that Kristin invest a healthy portion of her after-tax income. And as a person who'd seen tragedy strike so many times, Delilah arranged for Kristin to take out an insurance policy that would secure her future in case tragedy caused her to become unemployed because of disfigurement.

Aunt Delilah didn't consider herself a seer, but she was intuitive. She was proven all too right when after four meteoric years Kristin's modeling career abruptly ended and the rubble of her life made sensationalistic reading for a week or two in every tabloid in the country.

Reading the weekly pulp publications had been like reliving the assault each time the details were disclosed. They detailed the incredible story of a disheveled young man, a wild-eyed drifter, an obsessed fan, who had stalked Kristin, fantasizing that if she just saw him for a few minutes he could convince her of his love and she would return his feelings and they would live happily ever after. . . .

Instead, when he approached her on the street when she was alone, frightened, and distracted, she'd casually brushed him off. How was she to know that such rejection would provoke unrestrained rage and his attitude that if he couldn't have her, he'd see to it that no one would want her either!

She felt the hot, searing slash of the straight-edge razor almost before she had time to recognize the weapon.

The rest was a blur. She remembered screaming and screaming, cupping her face as her life's blood cascaded between her clutching fingers, causing horrible dark blotches to fall to the dusty gray cement sidewalk. She stood there surrounded by people who suddenly seemed not to want to become involved and rushed on by.

The huge insurance settlement was no consolation for the loss of her career and the pain inflicted each time she looked into a mirror. The money did however afford her the services of the best doctors available, as they attempted to put her face back together knowing they would never be able to repair her career.

While undergoing reconstructive surgery Kristin holed up in Dee's apartment, subletting her apartment to Janice and her new husband, an older man, a Wall Street stockbroker.

Aunt Dee was dating an executive from a foreign company,

who wanted her to marry him and live abroad. One doctor told her that Kristin's outer scars would heal. The doctor spoke cautiously of inner scars causing more serious disfigurement. He suggested that Kristin might want to seek help from a counselor, or perhaps a member of the clergy.

When the doctor released Kristin from his care, Aunt Delilah freed her, too, declaring her niece well enough and financially stable, to the point where Dee could marry her impatient suitor and make a life for herself abroad.

Kristin, not about to become a burden to anyone or rely on others any longer, agreed with a smile.

Alone, jobless, with no one to talk to about her fears and recurring nightmares, Kristi was unable to bear the city any longer. She slept poorly, lurching awake each time there was an odd scrape or bump in the night, and she felt like a nervous wreck, losing weight from her already slim figure. Andre and his staff had sent her flowers and visited her several times, telling her to come by the agency and see everyone. But it was clear that she was a has-been at age twenty-one.

Briefly Kristin returned to her old hometown, northwest of Chicago, but everything seemed changed. Old girlfriends had moved away. Or they'd married and were involved with their husbands and new babies. Or they were engaged and planning their weddings. It was embarrassing to Kris when hometown people still asked for her autograph, shoving old issues of magazines bearing her likeness on the cover in her face for her to sign.

And then there were the dreamy-eyed, insatiable teenage girls asking for details about her old, glamorous life and seeking advice on how they could attain fame and fortune just as the older girl-next-door had done.

But the worst were well-intentioned people, many of them shirttail relatives, who leaned forward and peered into Kristin's face, patting her arm as they pronounced the scars were "hardly visible unless you knew just where to look," adding that given time the lines would fade even more.

Kristin wanted only to forget the assault. She wanted to block out those years of her life. And she realized that the only way she could start over was to start fresh. Camden Corners, at the edge of Shawnee National Forest, where she'd once camped as a young girl, seemed the ideal choice.

But now, just as she was growing comfortable with her new life, old specters from the past arose to haunt her.

She'd been in front of the camera so many times that she'd not even allowed herself to be photographed since after her reconstructive surgery. The cosmetic surgeon's photographer had taken pictures of her when Dr. Steinberg considered his work complete. He wanted a before-and-after pictorial to attest to his expertise and assure subsequent patients that he could work miracles for them, too.

There was no way Kristin was going to go before a clicking shutter again. If it was impossible to receive the five thousand dollar check without getting her picture taken, they could just keep their money—and for that matter, the dude ranch trip, too!

She didn't need the money. But, elderly Mrs. Stanwyck was right, and she could use a vacation. . . .

*Mrs. Stanwyck!*

It had to have been her—Kristin's Thursday afternoon client—she realized, and her regularly Sunday morning companion at worship services.

The mysterious individual who'd entered her name in a sweepstakes box surely was Mrs. Stanwyck, who claimed that clipping coupons, snipping off proof-of-purchases seals, filling out refund forms, penning contest entries, and sending off for brochures, information, and free samples filled a lot of otherwise lonely, boring, unproductive hours. The widow of a one-time area pastor, Mrs. Stanwyck claimed the activities did wonders for the arthritis in her hands by keeping her fingers limber while ensuring her mind was active and alert. It gave her something to look forward to in the mail, she said, plus, it provided her a source of incoming stamps to save for mission projects and a dream to call her own.

And Mrs. Stanwyck was a firm believer in nurturing dreams.

Kristin sighed. Then she laughed with irony and a touch of affection when she found that she couldn't be angry with the elderly widow who'd come to seem like a grandmother to her. After all, Kristing was a young woman who felt as if she had no family, what with Aunt Dee in Europe and a mercenary Janice now relieved of Husband Number One and making it clear she was actively seeking a candidate for Spouse Number Two, provided the appropriate financial profile was provided upon application!

No one aside from dear Mrs. Stanwyck had considered that Kristin had been working for a year without any vacation and no mention of one, either.

Kristin had known that the old woman was concerned. But she hadn't realized to just what extent until that moment, and she was touched over such tangible evidence of another's caring.

A vacation wasn't all that Kristin's Thursday client had made clear she believed the younger woman could put to good use. An empathetic Mrs. Stanwyck probably thought that Kristin Allen needed money. So she'd frequently recommended her services to trusted friends.

An opinionated, unbending romantic, Mrs. Stanwyck believed that Kristin Allen could also use a boyfriend—and handed down the  tart verdict that Kristin's vicarious enjoyment of romantic novels and stories didn't count—and what she needed was a good man. A Christian man, of course, because in Mrs. Stanwyck's mind, none other would do. . . .

A pragmatic Mrs. Stanwyck had obviously concluded that Kristin could use a vacation—ideally in a place abounding with handsome, down-to-earth, hardworking men. So quite clearly Mrs. Stanwyck had given it her best shot and filled out who knew how many entry stubs in the slim hope that Kristin would win. . . and no doubt praying over the matter, trusting in God to come through with a miracle of sorts that would propel Kris into the path of Mr. Right.

❧

The next twenty-four hours found Kristin's telephone line frequently busy. She conferred with representatives of Happy Trails Horse Feed, the staff of the Circle K Dude Ranch, made tentative flight plans with a travel agent, and confirmed that it *had* been Mrs. Stanwyck behind her becoming a Grand Prize Winner.

On impulse Kristin had invited the woman out to dinner and they'd gone out for a pleasant meal then returned to the senior citizen's apartment complex on Sycamore Street. Her residence was just blocks away from the church and parsonage where her husband had pastored for most of his lifetime, and where Kristin attended services regularly.

Mrs. Stanwyck asked Kristin in for a cup of coffee. "I have had a wonderful evening, dear. I really appreciated it."

"It was the least I could do to thank you. I enjoyed it, too," Kristin said.

"We should go out more often."

"Maybe. That sounds nice. We will for sure after I get back from South Dakota. I'll have so much to tell you, I'm sure."

"I'll miss you, Kristin. But knowing that you're on vacation and having fun will be a comfort to me," Mrs. Stanwyck said. "And just think of what you can do with five thousand dollars, honey."

"That's something that I've been meaning to discuss with you," Kristin said, feeling suddenly hesitant and searching for tactful words. "I know that you want me to go to South Dakota. But I have decided that I won't go unless *you* accept the prize money check. If you won't agree to take the money, I won't go to the dude ranch."

Mrs. Stanwyck stared, shocked. "I. . .I'm afraid that I don't understand. Honey, I *want* you to have the money. You work so hard. You're young. Why, with five thousand dollars you could—"

Kristin lifted a hand to halt further speech.

"I know that I can trust you to keep a confidence," she said. "The truth is, I don't need the money. I'm financially secure without working. I have my Roving Maid business so that I can fill my hours. It makes me feel as if my life is still worthwhile when I help people by doing what they're not longer able to perform."

"I'm afraid that I don't understand," Mrs. Stanwyck said, frowning. But by the time Kristi finished explaining about her parents' deaths and the value of their estate that had been kept in trust for Kristin, and her sister, her career, and the insurance settlement, Mrs. Stanwyck understood perfectly.

"You'll agree to accept the check?" Kristin pressed for a commitment when she finished her explanations.

Mrs. Stanwyck, who lived on limited means, nodded. "If that's what it takes to get you to the Circle K Dude Ranch."

"Super," Kristin said, relieved, and gave her friend a hug. "Now we'll both be winners. We've had such fun tonight, wouldn't you like to go to the Circle K Dude Ranch for two weeks? It is a trip for two, you realize."

Mrs. Stanwyck laughed. "If I were twenty years younger, honey, I'd be buying boots and a ten gallon hat. You'd have to lasso me and tie me down to keep me home. Just looking at the brochure from the Circle K Ranch and seeing the exciting events awaiting you there, almost makes me have to reach for my nitro-glycerin pills."

"You've got a brochure?" Kristin said, surprised. "For the Circle K Dude Ranch?"

"Oh, yes, I'm almost positive that I do. It's around here somewhere. Probably in the box of travel brochures I've collected from agencies, and some that I sent off for after reading ads in travel magazines. You know me, always sending off for one thing or another. Would you like me to look for it?"

"If it's not too much trouble. The staff at the Circle K is sending me information, but I'd love a sneak preview."

"We could do it right now. Let me get my box of goodies," Mrs. Stanwyck said. "You can put the coffee on to percolate. We can sort through the pamphlets together."

"I'll be with you in a jiffy," Kristin called from the kitchen.

"Here it is!" Mrs. Stanwyck crowed within five minutes and triumphantly waved a glossy, full-color brochure. She took a quick peek, then handed it across to Kristin. "This is even better than I remembered!"

Kristin opened the pamphlet. A collage of pictures vied for her attention. It showed the ranch headquarters, the dining hall, the indoor recreation area and square dance auditorium, the chapel, gift shop, the rodeo chutes, the riding area, a corral full of pleasure horses, a herd of wild horses thundering across the pasture, a swimming pool, a lounge, spa facilities, children playing, and happy, suntanned, glowing people everywhere.

Kristin read the captions, then studied the pictures.

"Are those ranch hands handsome, or are they handsome?" Mrs. Stanwyck said, sighing.

"V. . .very handsome," Kristin said, and felt a strange tightness come to her chest as a warmth flowed to her cheeks. She hoped the pictures had not been posed by professional models but were actually candid photos of the real staff who worked at the Circle K Dude Ranch.

"South Dakota. . .a place where men are men," Mrs. Stanwyck said, "and by the looks of those handsome cowboys, know how to treat a lady like a woman. Kristin Allen, your life may never be the same again. At least that's what we can pray for."

Kristi gave an embarrassed laugh. "There's absolutely nothing wrong with my life right now."

"You've got a nice life, I'll grant you that, except for your distinct lack of a man to love—and a good, upstanding man Christian man who loves you. This vacation, my beautiful young friend," she said in an optimistic tone, as her eyes sought the brochure and centered on the chapel, "may offer just the solutions to those problems."

"Now let's not let our expectations get unrealistically high," Kristin warned.

Mrs. Stanwyck was thoughtful for a moment.

"Who are you going to ask to go with you, Kristin?"

Kristin shrugged. "Since you won't accompany me, I really have no one to ask but my sister."

"Janice?"

"Yes. The one and only."

At that moment Kristin wasn't so sure that she wanted to invite Jan, but she was even less sure that she could bear going to a dude ranch all by herself.

"It's been awhile since you've seen her?"

"Not since I moved back to Illinois. We talk occasionally. But our lives have moved in different directions. We've little in common nowadays except for the same relatives."

"There are few things as wonderful as close family ties. Traditions of faith. The wonderful memories we share with those we love. The special bonds created when He gives us to each other in families who share the same ancestors."

"I know. And that's something I've missed since. . .Mother and Dad died. . . ." Kristin brushed her hair away from her face as she found herself unable to go on. A lump that seemed the size of South Dakota suddenly lodged in her throat. "Asking Jan to go with me might be an ideal chance for us to start acting—and feeling—like family again."

"It's a step in the right direction. If she's any kind of sister, Kristin, she'll meet you half way and there'll be an end to any estrangement that's occurred."

"I think I'll go home right now and give Jan a call," Kristin said, feeling a sudden surge of enthusiastic optimism.

Ten minutes later Kristin let herself into her home, snapped on a lamp, reached for the telephone, looked up Janice's number and tapped in the sequence.

She tried to recall just when they'd talked last, a perfunctory, obligatory call to be certain. Christmas? Easter? New Year's? A birthday? Kristin realized that she was not sure.

Jan answered on the fourth ring, and Kristin explained who she was—twice—before Janice comprehended that it was her sister on the line.

Kristin winced when she detected that Janice sounded almost disappointed. At that instant she wished she hadn't even decided to call her big sister, but it was too late.

"The reason I'm phoning," Kristin got right down to business when they seemed to quickly run out of idle pleasantries, "is because I've had the most incredible thing happen to me. I won the Grand Prize in a sweepstakes—"

"Terrific, kiddo," Janice said. "Your best move is to contact the sweepstakes officials, tell them that you don't want the merchandise, and then dicker with them for a cash payoff instead of the cars, furs, diamonds, television sets or whatever they're awarding you."

"But I—"

"They may make you settle for less than the retail value of the items, because they'll get them at wholesale or for the benefit of advertising value, but with cash you're money ahead and you then have liquid funds to take care of the state and federal tax bills due on the amount without—"

"I didn't call for advice!" Kristin quickly spoke up when her sister paused for breath.

"Oh. Then what did you want?"

"Well, my prize is a vacation trip for two at a dude ranch," Kristin began. "I thought that perhaps you'd like to join me for two weeks. It would give us time together so that we can catch up on each other's lives again, and—"

"Oh, I'm sorry, Kristin, but that's not possible. I did a dude ranch right after Bernard and I split up a year ago, and I'm not in the market for that kind of diversion, not after what I went through when a girlfriend and I dallied with the cowboys. I promised myself: *never again!*"

"Oh." Kristin knew that she sounded as deflated as she felt. Janice seemed not to notice.

"But if you ever win a trip to Hawaii, Rio, Tahiti, the Riviera, Europe, or some place that's nice—by all means give me a ring, darling. I'll be packed and ready to go before we can end the call!"

Miserably Kristin fingered the brochure. "The Circle K Dude Ranch looks very nice," she murmured to fill the blossoming silence.

"Oh, I'm sure it is. Circle K? That sounds familiar. It could be the spread Cissy and I stayed at. But probably not," Janice dismissed. "You know how all of those ranch names get to sound alike after awhile."

"Yes," Kristi agreed, and she tried to think of a quick way to end the call that she wished she'd never made.

"Don't get me wrong," Janice said, with sudden warmth as she seemed to realize that the call was fast falling apart. "You'll have a wonderful time. You always were more of a tomboy and girl-next-door than I was. There are lots of things to do on a dude ranch—if you like that kind of activity and don't mind getting dirty, sweaty, sunburned, saddle sore. Oh, the agony of remembering," she said, groaning.

"I thought it looked like a lot of fun."

"And there are guys beyond compare if you go for the rugged, outdoorsy, taciturn type."

"I've seen the brochure. I hope they aren't professional models," Kristin said.

"Trust me. You're in luck. They aren't."

"That's nice to know," Kristi said and felt her spirits lift.

"But you'd better watch out for those dude ranch dudes," Janice offered a worldly warning. "And for Pete's sake, little sister, don't believe everything they tell you. Those cowboys are probably paid to treat every female guest as if she's Miss America, even if she's old, ugly, fat, and worthy of nothing but a healthy dose of pity."

*Or scarred?* Kristin helplessly added to the list.

"So don't swallow their romantic banter," Janice blithely reminded. "Why, it's very likely memorized repartee, with them having to pass an oral test before they're even hired on!"

"I'm sure I can recognize a line if I hear one. I'm hardly immature and irresponsible," Kristin said, feeling defensive, unable to prevent the chill that entered her tone.

"Well, in my estimation, my dear, you *are* inexperienced for a woman of your age, with your nose in a book when the rest of us discovered boys. And smiling at a camera when we moved on to learn how to deal with men. I don't want to see you hurt. I've been to a dude ranch, don't forget; I've seen the moves those cowboys put to the female guests."

"Do I hear the voice of experience talking?" Kristin muttered, not bothering to hide her needling sarcasm.

"Absolutely!" Janice assured, not even taking offense.

And then, as Kristin listened, held a captive audience, Janice told her about the rich and handsome cattleman who'd wooed her when she was a guest at the dude ranch his family owned.

"Talk about a whirlwind courtship," Janice said. "He was talking marriage almost before I'd unpacked my bags. I couldn't believe he was serious—for I certainly wasn't out for anything but a good time. He was wealthy enough, interesting, educated, and he could've had his pick of the women, and he made clear that he wanted me. But believe me, little sister, I didn't want him—or that horrible, prissy churchgoing mother and family of his. Believe me, I'd have taken that out of him soon enough and had him sleeping late on Sunday mornings, too. I didn't want what he had to offer enough to move to the wilderness, put up with his mother, brothers, and sisters, plus live on a

ranch in the boondocks where they had cows, horses, rattlesnakes, and I'd have to drive miles and miles to attend a
so-called cultural event that would've been laughed out of New
York City. And not only that, but he wanted children, too. . . .
Several." Jan gave a brittle laugh and shudder. "Can't you just
see me as *a mother?!*"

The way Jan's tone dropped in disgust, Kristin knew that
she'd just wrinkled her nose in distaste, and Kristin thanked
God that a child had been spared being born to her cold-hearted
big sister.

"I had no idea you'd had a dude ranch romance," Kristi said
as she prepared to end the call.

"We really *have* grown apart, haven't we? We never get a
chance to talk any more. But do listen to your big sister, huh?
I wouldn't lead you wrong, so mark my words about dude
ranches."

"Have you heard anything from Aunt Dee?" Kristi quickly
asked, changing the subject from Janice's mercenary love life
before she could warm to it again while Kristin's toll charges
ticked away.

"She and Uncle are due to arrive in New York within the
month. They'll be staying at the Plaza. Give me a call when
you're at the dude ranch, so I'll have a number where Aunt
Dee can reach you when she's stateside."

"Okay," Kristin agreed. "I'll do that."

"Good to talk to you, dear. We really *must* start staying in
touch. . . ."

"I'll call you from South Dakota," Kristin promised.

"Good enough, Kristi. Enjoy yourself. And remember what
I said, now: *be on guard!*"

## two

To Kristin's relief the flight from Lambert Field in St. Louis left on time, under excellent flying conditions. She realized her flight would be on time to Rapid City, South Dakota, where the staff from the Circle K Dude Ranch were waiting to take arriving guests to the ranch.

It was not a direct flight, but it seemed like they'd scarcely departed St. Louis airspace before the pilot instructed them to prepare for landing in Omaha, Nebraska. Although a flurry of passengers disembarked, Kristin remained in her seat. A number of people boarded the craft to continue on to the Rapid City Regional Airport.

Kristin had been involved in a novel she'd purchased at the gift shop at Lambert Field until the pilot taxied to the gate in Omaha, and the sunlight slanting through the window glared in her eyes. She retrieved wraparound sunglasses from her purse, slipped them on, and was content to watch people from behind the mirrored lenses. She watched as a mother and child took the seat ahead of her, and smiled politely, offering help, as the woman confronted difficulty with her child's safety restraint.

Kristin's attention was drawn forward in the cabin when the flight attendant greeted a man as if he were an old friend and asked him how rodeo competition had gone for him.

Kristin didn't hear his reply, but from the championship belt buckle at his waist and the triumphant grin on his tanned face, Kristin suspected that it had gone very well.

His eyes were incredibly blue, turquoise like the brilliant Nebraskan sky. As he sought his seat, for a moment he faced

Kristin and she was struck by how handsome he was.

Hair as black as her own, thick and wavy, the kind that seemed to beg a woman to sift her fingers through it, was topped by an expensive Stetson.

The man was tall, much taller than Kristin, broad-shouldered, lean, but solidly muscled. His jeans were faded and fit him almost like a second skin, and his tailored plaid western shirt with pearl buttons skimmed his trim torso. Top-of-the-line custom-made Tony Lama cowboy boots proved that he didn't mind paying for quality and comfort. And a light thatch of chest hair, peeking from the V of his casually unbuttoned shirt, was so blatantly masculine that Kristin felt oddly overwhelmed by the force of his presence.

For a moment their eyes met, or would have, if his glance hadn't been reflected back at him via her mirrored lenses. Then he looked through her and was gone, leaving Kristin realizing that she'd been holding her breath in awe.

If he was an indication of what the Western States, South Dakota in particular, had to offer, Kristin thought with amusement, she probably should've borrowed some heart medicine from Mrs. Stanwyck, for just the sight of him had done strange and wonderful things to her pulse!

Minutes later the flight attendant gave them the prepared departure speech and wished them a pleasant flight. A moment later the jet engines whined, the airplane began to move forward, and then catapulted ahead as momentum pressed them back in their seats. Suddenly they were airborne as down below everything became smaller and smaller.

For awhile Kristin read from her novel, but soon she slipped the book into her handbag and glanced out the side window so that she could admire the rugged terrain.

Kristin recalled what she'd learned about the region earlier in high school and linked it with what she saw spread out below. She and the other passengers leaned ahead, craning to look out their windows and catch sight of landmarks the pilot mentioned as he entered the airspace of Rapid City South Dakota.

Kristin marveled at the Black Hills National Forest, heavily forested mountains called the *Paho Sapa* by the Sioux Indians because of the terrain's pine-dark woods. Also in the general area was Mount Rushmore, that Kristin viewed from the air, but couldn't fully appreciate. She knew that the tourists down below at the observation point could as they gazed up at the likenesses of George Washington, Thomas Jefferson, Theodore Roosevelt, and Abraham Lincoln. The sculptures were seventy feet high and positioned six hundred feet above the valley floor, chiseled in granite.

The pilot explained that mining was important to the local industry, and he pointed out sightseeing points: the South Dakota School of Mines and Technology, the Museum of Geology, the Federal Sioux Indian Museum, Dinosaur Park, Black Hills Reptile Garden, Wild Cat Cave, Nameless Cave, and Badlands National Monument.

At the Rapid City Regional Airport, the pilot nosed the jet into the slot and workers rolled the ramp into place. Kristin arose, collected her carry-on belongings and moved into the aisle, filing out behind other passengers.

She went to the baggage carousel and waited patiently for her possessions. When she collected her second valise, she turned away just in time to see the handsome rodeo rider passing through the plate glass doors into the parking lot.

She felt a sense of loss that she would never see him again.

"Anyone else here happen to be going to the Circle K Dude Ranch?" a harried, slightly plump, ginger-haired, freckle-faced young woman asked.

"Yes, I am," Kristin replied, as did several others.

"Great!" the girl said, moving to Kristin's side, no doubt because they were approximately the same age and both by themselves. "Let's stick together. Okay?"

"Good idea," Kristin agreed. "There's supposed to be a van

from the ranch to meet us."

"We'll find it," the girl said in a confident tone. "My name's Amanda Gentry. My friends call me Mandy."

"I'm pleased to meet you. I'm Kristin Allen. Friends call me Kristi or Kris or Kristin."

"Call you anything, but don't call you late for lunch, eh?" the round-faced girl teased. Then she frowned. "As slim as you are, you probably don't have a problem with your weight."

"I've eaten my share of cottage cheese and lettuce," Kristin admitted, as suddenly her thoughts flicked back to the old days in New York when she'd had to deny herself so much for the sake of her career.

"In your case it's been worth it," Mandy murmured. "You've got a figure a lot of women would die for. Your face isn't bad, either. You know, for some reason, you really look familiar to me. Have we met?"

At Mandy's remark about her face, Kristin felt as if she'd been slapped, but then realized the girl had meant nothing unpleasant, that it was simply her colloquial way of speaking.

"I. . .I don't think so," she managed to reply. "I'm sure I'd have remembered you."

"Hmmm. I'd almost swear that I've seen you before." Mandy gave her a closer look.

Suddenly Kristin felt self-conscious. She turned away, not wanting to see Mandy scrutizing her scars, if that's what she was doing, even though Mrs. Stanwyck had assured her that Dr. Steinberg's handiwork was so good that a stranger wouldn't even know she'd once been severely disfigured.

"There I go again," Mandy sighed as silence stretched to the snapping point. "Ol' open-mouth-insert-foot Mandy. The girls in the typing pool and data processing area are used to me, so I forget that you're not."

Kristin managed a bright, warm smile. "But I soon will be. I'm sure we'll see each other around the Circle K spread. Got your bags, Mandy? Let's go."

"I'm glad we met," Mandy said. "I had reservations, no pun intended, about coming to the dude ranch all alone. But now that we've met, I feel like I've already got a friend."

"I know the feeling. Over there's the van," Kristin said.

"And there's an honest-to-goodness-rootin'-tootin'-cowboy. Help me, Kris." Mandy clutched in the area of her heart near where hung a golden cross on a delicate chain. "I think I'm in love!"

Kristin found herself laughing. "Better watch out, Mandy, or instead of the people at the Circle K Dude Ranch letting you have a vacation, they'll *hire* you."

"What are you talking about?"

"My sister came to a dude ranch last year and she said that the cowboys aren't to be trusted, that they have a line for every woman between eight and eighty. They rope, ride, rodeo, and *romance,* with equal skill. According to Janice they're absolutely not to be believed. Unfortunately. . . ."

Mandy curled a lip then gave a flip grin. "Oh, who cares?" she joyously asked. "I came here to have a healthy helping of fantasy. I have enough reality back at the office in Kirkwood, Missouri. Cruise ship romances don't seem to last, either. So what? Enjoy it while it lasts, eh?"

The two girls approached the large white van that had the logo of the Circle K Dude Ranch emblazoned on the side. A pleasant ranch hand with a welcoming attitude was greeting the spread's guests, stowing luggage, and directing them inside to find seats in the air-conditioned vehicle.

"Hi, girls!" he greeted Mandy and Kristin as they approached.

"Hello, there!" Mandy boldly replied, grinning, while Kristin offered a demure smile.

The smile froze on her face when the employee of the Circle K Ranch regarded her, did a double take, and gave her an odd and seemingly displeased stare. He looked at her as if he expected her to say something, then as if he considered making a remark himself, but thought better of it.

Without another glance at either of them he tossed the girls' luggage into the hold, and brusquely gestured them into the van.

"He must have a burr under the saddle," Mandy muttered. "Oh well, he's not the only cowboy in the Wild West, even if he is awfully cute."

The suddenly taciturn ranch employee stood outside a moment, tallied up the guest sheet, concluded that everyone was present and accounted for, and that they could proceed east from Rapid City to the Circle K Ranch. The driver wended through traffic and departed the terminal area, passed the Pennington County Fairgrounds, then took the entrance ramp onto Interstate 90. Initially the traffic was thick, but as they left the immediate Rapid City vicinity, it thinned. Mandy kept up a constant flow of chatter, and Kristin was grateful that she'd connected with the easy-to-like, outgoing, obviously fun-loving girl.

So far her trip was fantastic. If only she could figure out why the nice-looking cowboy from the Circle K, who'd had a distinctly reserved attitude, cool, actually, when he dealt with Mandy and her, kept looking at her in the rearview mirror, sneaking peeks, then quickly pulling his eyes away when Kristin's gaze happened to catch his in the mirror.

"Va-va-va-voom!" Mandy sighed. "Would ya look at *that!*"

Kristin glanced down to where Mandy's brown-eyed gaze lingered and she saw a cowboy, not just any cowboy, but *the rodeo champion cowboy*, cruising alongside the van in a white Corvette.

"I'm in love!" Mandy moaned for the second time in what seemed a matter of minutes. "I wish the driver of this van would peddle a little bit faster! I don't want to lose sight of that 'Vette!"

As if on cue the driver of the Corvette gave a jaunty tap on his horn, the cowboy in control of the ranch's van beeped back, gave a friendly wave, and then the cowboy in the Corvette accelerated and sped ahead.

"Oh, giddyap, buster!" Mandy complained at the driver under her breath. "Don't spare the horses under the hood up there. Or back here. Or wherever the engine in this ol' van is!"

"Too late, Mandy," Kristin said. "He's gone."

"But not forgotten. I may remember that face when I'm old and gray. Oh well, this is South Dakota," the Missourian sighed.

"'Where men are men, and know how to treat a lady like a woman,' a friend of mine told me," Kristin added.

The idea lifted Mandy's spirits.

"I'm in heaven!" the vacationing computer operator announced.

Twenty minutes later Mandy repeated the remark when the van's driver slowed to negotiate a long, winding drive that led to the headquarters of the Circle K Dude Ranch.

Both girls swiveled around, as did other passengers, to take in all that the dude ranch had to offer.

There was a large main building that housed the offices, lobby, dining room, square dance auditorium, chapel, beauty shop, gift boutique, indoor swimming pool, game room, and western wear store. Outdoors there were tennis courts, a mini-golf course, corrals, riding arenas, a pool, chaise lounges, patio tables, and an assortment of playground equipment for children.

Pristine sidewalks bordered by bright flower beds led to the various compounds where there were units large enough to house complete families and quarters ideal for a person alone.

"What a place," Mandy sighed. "I hope our rooms won't be too far apart. Oh! That's mine!" she sang out as the van's driver flipped a luggage label and called out her name.

"Kristin Allen?"

"Over here," she said and moved forward to collect her bags.

The cowboy consulted the luggage label, looked into Kristin's eyes as if he'd had trouble reconciling the face with the name, then he handed over her bags.

"Have a nice stay, Ma'am," he murmured and gave her such

a warm smile that her heart skipped a beat. She felt ever so much better after enduring his coldly hostile glances in the rearview mirror for the last forty miles.

"I'm sure I will," she replied in a friendly tone.

Mandy was waiting for her. "Well, ol' Stoneface finally softened up enough to smile at you, eh?" she whispered, leaning close to Kristin. "I wonder what his problem was?"

"I don't know. But whatever it was, he must've solved it."

"Unless your sister's right, and it is a bought-and-paid-for act and now that he's at the headquarters he knows he's got to mind his p's and q's because Big Brother is watching."

"Oh, I don't think so," Kristin said. "It could've been something as simple as a headache."

"You're right. We're all entitled to a bad day now and then."

"It's such a long line waiting in the lobby to check in, Mandy, what do you say that we wait on that bench over in the shade and enjoy the scenery?"

"Sounds good. It might increase our chances of getting rooms near each other, too."

Fifteen minutes later the girls entered the lobby. Mandy excused herself to go to the restroom while Kristin saw to her reservation.

The desk clerk, who Kristin had watched pleasantly deal with the other guests, looked up, and gave her a friendly, generic smile before he'd seemed to focus on her as an individual. When he did, the man's expression seemed to chill ten degrees.

He gave her a barely perceptible nod of greeting.

"Alone this year?" he murmured.

"Yes, I'm afraid so," Kristi said politely. "The name is—"

"Let me see about your—" The man's words trailed off as he riffled through the file box bearing alphabetized reservation cards without even bothering to hear her out. He frowned, but then looked almost gloating. "I'm sorry, but we don't seem to have you registered. Perhaps there's space at the motel in town—"

Kristin's heart leaped to her throat. "Oh dear, that can't be! I made the arrangements myself. I received the confirmation card, although I didn't bring it with me. C. . .could you check again? Please? The name is Kristin Allen. I. . .I'm the person who won two weeks here as Grand Prize Winner of the Happy Trails—"

"Oh, Ms. *Allen* is it? I'm sorry; my mistake," the man said. He flipped to a different section of the file box. "I don't know where my mind was. I had you confused with a guest I remembered from last year, also a very. . .uh. . .pretty young woman. Ah, here we are. And everything *is* in order, I'm relieved to discover. Sorry about that, Ma'am."

Quickly, efficiently, and with genuine warmth, he executed the paperwork and Kristin was affixing her signature when Mandy reappeared.

"Anything else I can do for you, Ms. Allen?" he asked helpfully, as if to make up for the fact that things had gotten off to a poor start.

"Well, if you can put my new friend in quarters close to mine, I know that we'll both be grateful."

"I can put you in rooms right beside each other."

"Super!" Mandy said and favored him with a grin.

Kristin smiled happily. "You can't get any better than that!"

"One of the hands will come for your luggage and show you to your rooms," the desk clerk said. "And tonight to welcome our guests we're having a Texas-style barbecue done up to South Dakota specifications."

Mandy rubbed her tummy. "I *am* in heaven," she whispered to Kristin. "Let them show me to my room, show me me where the cowboys are, and point me toward the barbecue pit."

The girls got settled in their quarters, freshened up, changed clothes, and decided to walk around to see what diversions the dude ranch offered. Then they wandered toward the barbecue pit. Delicious aromas crowded the air.

Eventually other guests began arriving, and the festive

event began.

The food was excellent, the companionship enjoyable, and as fireflies flickered in the dusky twilight, an area band tuned up their guitars, fiddles, and banjos. Toe-tapping, foot-stomping square dance rhythms filled the cool night air.

People that Kristin realized were area ranch families had been invited to the big celebration to make the city dudes feel welcome. Handsome cowboys of all ages approached women, asking them to dance, while cute local cowgirls took visiting city boys in hand.

There were giggles and protests, but these were met with the assurance that anyone could at least learn to do the simple two-step, that they were there to have a great vacation, and there was no time like the present to get started on enjoying themselves.

Mandy and Kristin were approached and found themselves led to the pavilion with an outdoor dance floor. Mandy was giggling, but giving it her all, and Kristin followed suit. The handsome young ranchers stayed with the girl from Camden Corners and the typist from Kirkwood, and they spent a memorable evening listening to the rollicking Country and Western music.

Mandy seemed to really like the young cowboy, Billy Joe, who was teasing her and sticking close as a burr. And while Kristin liked the young man, Kerry Kendrick, who was about her age and a student studying mechanics at a technical institute, she could tell that he was liking her a little too much. The way he was regarding her definitely wasn't bought and paid for by the hour by the big boss of the Circle K Dude Ranch. . . .

Kristi liked Kerry Kendrick. In fact, she liked him enough that she didn't want to risk hurting his feelings by seeming to string the kind, flawlessly mannered, quiet young cowboy along. So she'd eventually end up telling him that she wasn't as attracted to him as he seemed to be to her.

In the back of her mind she wondered if she was finding

fault with his youthful exuberance so she could make excuses to cut any ties with him before she could find herself involved and unsure of how to proceed. Or if it was simply a lack of that special chemistry. Or perhaps, even, that she often felt old beyond her years from what she'd had to face as a teenager, and because she'd worked and mingled with people so much older than she that she wasn't truly comfortable with people generally considered in her peer group.

When Kristin saw a teenager, with a thick head of deep auburn hair, and intense brown eyes, looking incredibly sad as all around her people were so happy, Kristin suggested that Kerry invite the girl to dance.

"I don't want to monopolize your time," she said in a light tone, "and that little girl looks like she'd love to learn how to do a Texas two-step. You're an excellent tutor."

"Oh. . .okay," Kerry said. "If you're sure that you don't mind."

"Of course not. I have to go to my room for a few minutes."

"Okay. See you around, Kristin."

"Sure thing. And thanks for the lessons!"

Kristi threaded her way through the crowd.

"Leaving already?" Mandy cried, as Billy Joe swung her through a vigorous square dance and her face glowed with happiness.

"For a little while. I have some calls I should make."

"Hurry back!" Mandy cried after her.

As Kristin made her way from the pavilion her footsteps clacked along the sidewalk. She walked through the darkness from one dim carriage lamp to another and was not sure how far she'd gone before she realized that she was not alone.

Someone was walking behind her, rapidly gaining!

For a moment she felt terror ricochet through her as the full horror of the long-ago attack froze her mind before she forced herself to concentrate on the fact that she was at a secure dude ranch, surrounded by convivial vacationers, and that there was no one who wished her any harm.

She started to turn off the sidewalk to the path that led to the cluster of rooms where she and Mandy were housed, when a steel strong grip contained in a smooth leather riding glove snaked out, encircled her wrist, and yanked her back.

Kristin felt her knees grow weak and buckle, then a tall, lean, very strong, and very angry cowboy jerked her upright, lifting her face to within inches of his.

Kristin gasped, then tried to scream, but she was unable to even speak or make any sound. Her eyes widened with fright and she searched the dark for a clue to her attacker's identity.

She stared, stunned, when she saw that it was him. *Him!* The handsome rodeo rider from the flight to Dallas from Kansas City. The cowboy in the white Corvette!

Kristin was trying to collect herself to the point where she could form words and tell the cowboy to take his hands off her, but then his grip tightened and he pulled her into the shadows. He propped her against the clapboard building, leaning one arm against the wall, then glared down at her as she looked up.

He gave a cold smile that was followed by a bitter, cutting laugh. And his eyes that had been so turquoise on the airplane became like blue-white lightning flashing to cleave a thunderous summer sky.

"Had to return again, huh?" he drawled mockingly. "Just couldn't stay away? Couldn't leave well enough alone?" Then he seemed about to call her an unflattering name but managed to check himself.

"Please—" Kristin whispered, swallowing hard, as her throat was dry and tight with tension and she felt a heartbeat away from bursting into tears. "There's some kind of mistake—"

He gave another harsh laugh. "You'd better believe there's been a mistake. A passle of them, and most of 'em *mine!* Your reservation should've been refused! You should've been sent away bag and baggage. Haven't you done enough to this family? I saw you dancing and romancing my kid brother, Kerry.

Are you trying to get even with me through him?! Well, I'm warning you lady: stay away from him. I won't have you doing to him what you did to me. Thanks to how you turned my life upside down, I feel that I've all but lost my faith. That's what I get for being so foolish as to let my heart go counter to my head and think that I could have a decent life and healthy relationship yoked with an unbeliever."

"I don't know who you are, or what you're talking about—"

"Sure you don't!" The man said in a grating tone and gave Kristin a shake that convinced her to hold her silence.

"But if you think you're going to break Kerry's heart, the way you did mine, I won't let you get away with it. This time, you cold-hearted seductress. . .*I'll make you pay!* I know that vengeance is the Lord's, but cross me, sister, and mess up my little brother's heart and mind, and I'll exact my own revenge, too. And consider it as sweet as our relationship that went so sour!"

"Get away from me or I'll report you to the owner of this ranch!" Kristin flared.

For an answer the man laughed in her face.

"Go away and leave me alone!" Kristin ordered, feeling suddenly angry and frightened to the point of feeling competent to handle him and give as good as she got.

"Gladly," the cowboy said and gave a derogatory laugh. He jerked his touch away as if he'd been burned by her satiny flesh. "No man in his right mind would get within a country mile of a calculating vixen like you. After my father was killed in a rodeo accident, I promised my mother that I'd protect and help raise my brothers and sisters. Kerry's just a kid—a trusting kid—but he's *my responsibility* and I'm not going to have you wrecking him the way you tried to ruin me. Toy with his affections and beliefs, Janice, pretend that you're something special that you're not. It took me awhile to figure it out before I came to my senses. Try to get your hooks into the Kendrick money by latching onto Kerry, and you'll answer to me, Janice!"

A shocked Kristin was unable to frame a response, and she sagged with relief when the furious cowboy turned away, leaving her to collapse against the building for support.

"And don't bother going for any moonlight rides with the intention of showing up on my doorstep for old time's sake, either," he tossed another furious stricture over his shoulder. "I can't believe that I was once foolish enough to believe that I loved you." He fixed her with an impaling stare. "I'd sooner be horsewhipped and dragged for ten miles behind a stampeding mustang than spend another moment with you. . . ." He spat the scornful words into the velvety night.

And then he was gone leaving Kristin shaking.

What on earth was going on? she wondered.

A moment later she flinched and felt even more weak when she recalled that during his tirade, when she'd been too upset to speak, almost too nervous to think, he had called her *Janice*.

All the little clues that she'd encountered that day began to stack within her mind, building a case, from the cowboy looking through her when her features had been hidden behind sunglasses on the airplane, to the van's driver treating her with hostile indifference, to the room clerk gloating as he told her that she had no reservation, and the curious looks from ranch personnel as she and Mandy strolled the grounds.

Added to the fact that they all warmed, instantly and apologetically, when her true identity was revealed, convinced her that she'd been punished for another's cruel and selfish crimes.

*Janice's!*

# three

Kristin felt shaky and tense long after she let herself into her room, deadbolted the door, and secured the chain lock. She felt almost as if she were dreaming and wished that she could awaken to discover a different, less confusing, frustrating reality.

She'd hungered to see the cowboy in the white Corvette again, but most certainly not under the circumstances of their subsequent confrontation.

Trying to calm her nerves, methodically Kristin set about the ordinary unpacking, coordinating outfits, and putting her personal possessions in drawers for the next two weeks.

Soon she gave in to her impulse to call Janice. Kristin reminded herself that she had promised she'd pass along her telephone number so that Jan, Aunt Delilah, and Uncle Benchley could contact her when they were reunited in New York City.

It was a good excuse to dial Jan's number, although she had far more important business, the Corvette Cowboy, to discuss.

Kristin was disappointed when Janice's answering machine took the call. Resolutely she left her name, number, and a brief message that she'd had a pleasant flight to Rapid City.

Sighing, she replaced the receiver in the cradle just as there came a furtive tap at her door.

Kristin's heart leaped to a staccato beat. She crossed to the door, glanced through the peephole, then undid the various locks to allow Mandy to enter her quarters.

"I thought you were going to come back to the dance," Mandy said.

"I was going to," Kristin replied. "But something came up."

Mandy gave her an assessing stare and quirked an eyebrow. "Don't you mean *somebody*?"

"You saw. . . ."

Mandy nodded. "What a secret you were keeping from me. I never dreamed that you knew the Corvette Cowboy, Kris."

"I don't, Mandy. He's a stranger, and a rude one at that. It wasn't at all what it might have looked like to you. He wasn't hugging me, he was hurting me. I-I'm afraid of him. . . ."

"Afraid?" Mandy laughed, as if the idea were preposterous. Kristin's newfound friend searched her face, then plopped down on the neat bed. "You really are frightened," she breathed, dazed. "You're shaking with nerves."

"It wasn't pleasant, believe me," Kristin said in a low voice. "Today has been an ongoing nightmare. He, *they*, have all been mistaking me for someone else."

"Is *that* what's been going on?" Mandy murmured. Her brow drooped in consternation. "I'd noticed, Kris, how there didn't seem to be any happy medium for you. People here either loved you. . .or they seemed to. . .hate you."

"I know," Kristin's tone was bleak. "And believe me it's been upsetting. And the hot-tempered, short-fused, bullying Corvette Cowboy—"

"Dacian Kendrick's his name, by the way," Mandy inserted.

"—thinks that I'm a woman he used to be romantically involved with. And if *that's* any indication of how he treats a woman—"

Mandy almost swooned. "Oh, don't you wish. No, don't *I* wish. I saw him drag you into the shadows," she said, her voice growing husky.

"But how he behaved would not appeal to you. This Dacian Kendrick told me in no uncertain terms to stay away from his brother, Kerry."

"The other guy you were dancing with for most of the night?"

"One and the same."

"After delivering a scathing ultimatum, Mr. Kendrick left. He didn't actually hurt me, but he was threatening, and I don't trust him and certainly don't like him," Kristin said. "People who lose control and have a capacity for violence really upset me. I. . .I've been stewing over this ever since I came back to my room, trying to figure out what to do, Mandy. Do you think that perhaps I should report this Dacian Kendrick to the owner of the Circle K Ranch?"

Mandy looked stunned, then gave a shocked giggle before she began to explain. "Kris, you can't report him to the boss of the Circle K. Dacian Kendrick *is* the owner of this spread."

"In that case, maybe I'd better leave," Kristin said and arose, looking around her as if she didn't know what to repack first. "The way he feels about me—"

"No, silly girl, if it's been a case of mistaken identity it's not how he actually feels about *you*. It's how he thinks he feels about you because he doesn't know who you are and that's simply how he feels about the person he thinks you are. *Her!* So it's not how he really feels about *you*." Mandy paused and cleared her throat. "If you can follow that. . . ."

"Um. . .Perfectly. . . .I think. Do you by any chance have a Ph.D. in Illogic?"

Mandy grinned. "I haven't done my doctoral thesis yet. But seriously, Kris, it seems to me that the solution is to go to his office and tell him you're not who he thinks you are."

Kristin gave an adamant shake of her head. "I'm not going within one hundred yards of that man!"

Mandy quirked a brow. "Honey, if he *owns* this ranch, and if he's sitting in his office, you already *are* within a hundred yards of him."

"Do me a favor; don't remind me."

"I could do you a different favor," Mandy offered. "*I* could tell him you're not who he thinks you are." She didn't wait for Kristin to nix or approve the idea. "Who does he think you are, anyway?"

Kristin was about to tell her, but then she shrugged and shook her head.

Old habits were hard to break, and while she liked Mandy and felt comfortable with her, the needs for privacy and protection were too great. Plus, it would be embarrassing to have to admit to Mandy what kind of woman her big sister had obviously become.

"Who knows?"

"Obviously the way people have been giving you dirty looks and snubbing you all afternoon and evening, this despicable, unpleasant someone must look so much like you," Mandy mused, "that she could pass for your sister."

"It would seem so. Truly, Mandy, it might be simplest if I just packed my bags and in the morning arranged for someone to see me back to the airport and I'll return home."

"You can't do that to me, Kris!" Mandy protested. "Don't leave me all alone. We've been having such fun together. Please don't go. There's always tomorrow, and surely things will be better then. In fact, I know that. I've seen God take terrible situations and bring great good from them. I'll bet you've seen that happen too, no longer than it's been since you made the commitment to Christ as you were telling me about in the van from the airport."

Kristin was forced to nod in agreement. She would never forget that moment when after church with Mrs. Stanwyck, Sunday dinner together, and continuing on for an afternoon of talking of things of faith, she'd felt such hunger in her heart, and such hope, that she'd experienced to the core of her soul the knowledge that Jesus Christ, whom she scarcely had met, was her personal Savior and Lord.

Suddenly she wanted to know everything about Him, to understand His life, ministry and death upon earth, and the redemption found in Him. She'd felt frustrated—there'd been so much she wanted to know and understand, and she'd suffered human impatience, in realizing it would take *time* to discover the joys, depth, and maturity of faith.

Mrs. Stanwyck had chuckled and admonished her not to be impatient, but to trust in God to give her wisdom in His own way, and to know that He would teach her many lessons about faith in her daily walk with Him. The pastor's widow had warned her that she'd learn as much from human failure as she would from Christian triumph. She had said that sometimes the hard lessons that the Lord let us learn, through our own willfulness as we were in His permissive will instead of His perfect will, were those we'd look upon with the most gratitude as truths hard-won.

Kristin knew that suddenly she felt loved, cared for, fed spiritually, and nourished with Scripture while with her friends who were believers. She knew it in a way that worldly acquaintances couldn't ever hope to fill the void within her with any form of edification, for their ways were not those of people committed to God and to strengthening others who had placed their lives and trust in Him.

Could this be, as Mandy seemed to surmise, some kind of lesson from the Lord. . .for her? For Dace Kendrick, too?

Kristin nodded. "I suppose you're right. But if things aren't better within a day or two, I'm definitely leaving."

"The others figured out that you're not *her*, didn't they?" Mandy pointed out.

"Yes, the driver of the van suddenly got very nice when he saw my name on the luggage identification label. And so did the desk clerk."

"See?" Mandy assured. "Why, Dacian Kendrick might have already found out just how wrong he was about you."

"Maybe," Kristin said. "Although I'm not sure I care what that arrogant, egotistical, self-centered, bullying man believes."

"I still think he's perhaps the most handsome man I've seen

in all twenty-two years of my life," Mandy admitted. "And if he's anything at all like Kerry, he's probably actually very, very nice."

"That was my first impression of him. And my second impression, too. But if the third one's the charm—he was anything *but* nice," Kristin sourly enumerated.

Mandy smiled and yawned. "At least you can joke about it. That means you're getting better already. By tomorrow it'll have faded like a bad dream."

"It's been a long day for both of us," Kristin said. "Maybe tomorrow will be better."

"I'm going to hit the hay," Mandy said, yawning.

"Spoken like a true cowgirl."

"I'm trying," Mandy said. "And tomorrow, right after breakfast, this city gal's going to ask for a Heavy Duty Horse and learn how to ride."

"Meet me for breakfast, and we'll get adventurous together. I haven't been on a horse in years, although I used to love to ride when I was a child. After that I couldn't risk costly black and blue marks or even worse a broken arm or leg from a fall. I would like to get in a bit of fun before I may be. . .forced. . .to leave. . . ."

Kristin had felt significantly better after talking with Mandy and taking a long, hot, relaxing shower. Although she would've bet that she'd have been too keyed up to sleep, she drifted off within minutes of snuggling down in the comfortable bed.

She hadn't left a wake up call and the sun slanting through the windows, brightening the room, eventually awakened her.

She dressed, put on makeup, braided her long, black hair, then pulled it up, tucked the tips under, secured it with an ornate butterfly clip, donned her cowboy hat to protect her skin from the sun, and was ready to go.

She was checking her reflection in the mirror when there was a light tap on her door.

"Just a minute," she called.

She crossed to the door, expecting to see Mandy when she glanced through the peephole. She was not anticipating a spray of roses that all but hid the bearer's features.

"What on earth—?" she gasped as she opened the door.

"Ms. Kristin Allen?" The ranch employee asked, and Kristin nodded. "These are for you. The card's attached."

"Why. . .they're beautiful."

"Where do you want me to put them, Ma'am?"

"Over there on the table in front of the window would be wonderful."

The ranch employee did as instructed, smiled at Kristin, wished her a nice day, then turned to depart. Mandy was preparing to enter as the staff worker exited.

"Roses? You don't even have to tell me who they're from, Kris. I'll bet the flowers are from *him*. I told you he'd find out how wrong he was and be mortified. A dozen long-stemmed red roses? Obviously he was *very* embarrassed."

"As well he should be after his obnoxious behavior."

"We all make mistakes and need to forgive our trespasses as we would hope to be forgiven. So give the guy a break, Kris. And read the card. See what he has to say."

Kristin had freed the small card from the florist's envelope.

> *My Dear Ms. Allen:*
> *Apologetic words and flowers cannot convey to you the regret and embarrassment I suffered upon discovering that you were a perfect stranger, while I behaved like a perfect boor. Please accept this as a token of my apology until I can personally express my regrets.*
>
> > *Sincerely,*
> > *Dace Kendrick*

*P.S. For what I did to you perhaps I should be
horse-whipped and dragged for ten miles behind
a stampeding mustang. . . .*

Kristin gave an ironic laugh and handed the card to Mandy, who was unabashedly crowding close to see what it said.

She read it quickly. "What does the P.S. mean?"

"His parting words to me last night," she said. "He warned me not to show up on his doorstep for 'old time's sake,' because he said that he'd sooner 'be horsewhipped and dragged for ten miles by a stampeding mustang than spend another hour' with me."

"Not you, honey, *her*. Boy, she must've been some wicked number, huh? Wouldn't you give a pretty penny to know who she was?"

"Mandy, my dear," Kristin sighed, "I'd pay a small fortune to keep them all from finding out just who she is."

The remark seemed to take a moment to dawn. Mandy's eyes widened and her mouth dropped open. "You mean you *know*? Don't keep me in suspense like this! She must really be something to have gotten under Mr. Kendrick's skin like this."

"Believe me, she *is* something," Kristin said and took a deep, sighing breath. "I have a horrible feeling that the woman everyone loves to hate is none other than my big sister, Janice. And don't you dare tell a soul!"

"Wild horses couldn't drag it out of me!"

"Amanda Gentry. . .I think I'll pardon that pun if you don't mind," Kristin said in a weary voice. "Let's go get some breakfast, see about those horses, and forget all about the big boss man Dace Kendrick."

"Yeah," Mandy said. Her smile brightened. "He's not the only cowboy in South Dakota. Although he may be the most handsome. . . ."

Mandy was such a novice that the foreman in charge of the

corral singled her out for individual beginner's instructions. He sent for a big, gentle mare, Molly. Molly was brought from the neighboring residence for one month each summer because she was so sweet-natured and affectionate that she was a favorite of all the children who came to the Circle K for the two weeks reserved especially for youngsters each season.

Kristin, as a more advanced rider, was given Misty, a beautifully marked, dainty Appaloosa for her mount.

"I'll wait for you in the lounge area of the indoor riding arena," Mandy called after Kristin as Molly was brought out for the lesson to begin.

Two hours later Mandy limped out to meet Kristin and the other returning riders.

Kristin deftly dismounted and handed Misty's reins to a young man, one of many on the payroll, for him to curry, rub down, water, and walk after its use.

"How did your lesson go, Mandy?"

"I think I've figured out everything there is to know about horses. I watched the cowboys in a nearby corral practicing bronco busting on a mustang from the Kendrick's herd of wild horses. They're raised to sell to rodeo contractors."

"Oh? Do tell."

"One, they buck. Two, they bite. Three, they'll stomp on you. Four, they'll kick you when you're down. . . ."

"I saw Molly. She'd do no such things."

"Molly is an ol' sweetheart," Mandy agreed. "The lesson went very well, in fact, super, Jake says. But, maybe he's *paid* to tell all the greenhorns that. . . ."

"What'd you learn today?"

"How to mount up. Neck rain. And start and stop the horse." Kristin smiled. "Have trouble finding the blinkers?"

"Locating the horn and emergency brake were my big problems. Actually, I had a nice ride. Now I could use a swim. Or," she eased a manicured hand down her side to settle at the small of her back, "a whirlpool bath."

"I think there is one someplace. This ranch seems to offer just about everything."

"Before we go back to our rooms there's something you really should see, Kris. The Kendrick Family Rodeo Hall of Fame. Actually it is more like the Dacian F. Kendrick Hall of Fame. There are trophies that his father won. And his brothers. Even his sisters got barrel-racing and trick-roping awards. But it's clear that Dacian is the big rodeo talent in the family."

Kristin sighed so hard it riffled her bangs. "Dacian Kendrick! Is that all I'm going to hear today?"

"What's the matter with you? I was only making conversation and talking about my morning."

"I know, Mandy, and I'm sorry if I seem testy. But you're not the only one talking about Dacian Kendrick. Some of the other women along for the ride kept mentioning him and then the ranch employees sent along to babysit us on our maiden ride did nothing but sing his praises. Talk about hero worship! He seems much adored by everyone but Yours Truly."

"Ummm. Maybe we'll convert you yet. The guys in the arena and corral do seem to think he can do no wrong, too, now that you mention it."

"Maybe they're paid to say that. Believe me, Mandy, I could've opened up a few eyes if I'd opened my mouth about how he treated me last night!"

"He did send you flowers this morning and a note of apology."

"That doesn't change how I feel."

"He really hurt your feelings."

"You'd still be smarting, too, if it had happened to you, Mandy. And yes, he hurt my feelings. But worse, he scared me. I. . .I was attacked once," Kristin found herself opening up, even though she wasn't really sure that she wanted to. She threw caution to the wind and continued, "I was held against my will and wounded to the point where I was hospitalized and underwent corrective cosmetic surgery several times."

"How awful, Kris. . . ." Mandy's sympathetic face conveyed her deep dismay. "I had no idea. No wonder you were so shaken last night. An attack would leave you traumatized."

"Mr. Kendrick's actions last night brought back a lot of very unpleasant memories and feelings that I would rather not deal with. I just want to forget them now as I made myself put them from mind, suppress them, when it happened. I came here to have fun."

"We can skip the Hall of Fame."

"No. We're almost there. That way I can say that I've seen it," Kristin pointed out. "Coming to the Circle K and not visiting the Hall of Fame would be like going to Paris and ignoring the Eiffel Tower."

The girls wandered around the Hall of Fame that Mandy was viewing for the second time. Kristin, in spite of herself, was impressed.

When she forgot *whose* career she was admiring, she felt a sense of awe. And there was no missing how Dace Kendrick had gone from a sparkly-eyed, cute Little Britches rodeo contestant to become an adult Professional Rodeo Cowboy Association All-Star year after year, walking away with almost every award there was to be won at the biggest rodeo of them all in Oklahoma City.

Although she'd labeled him egotistical, there was a disconcerting expression of poignant humility in his eyes as photographers captured him accepting trophies, belt buckles, and silver-trimmed saddles.

"Quite a guy, isn't he?"

"He's had an impressive career."

"Although he's a rich man, Kris, he's been good to the working man of America," Mandy said. "Why, it's obvious that he's kept all kinds of smelters and metal workers employed producing trophies!"

Kristin laughed. "And probably someone local gainfully employed to dust them all."

Mandy gave Kristin a playful nudge in the ribs. "I'd be his Roving Maid any time."

Minutes later the girls were walking from the cool Kendrick Hall of Fame when the dinner bell clanged, ringing out through the noonday heat.

"Lunch already?" Mandy said and glanced up to check the sun's position.

"How time flies when you're having fun."

"Let's hurry and get cleaned up, chow down, and then go swimming," Mandy suggested.

"I don't know. As hot as it is I'd like to, but—"

"But what?" Mandy prompted when Kristin's voice trailed off.

"There'll probably be so many people in the pool as sunny and hot as it's going to be this afternoon."

"So? That's what the pool is there for."

"I know. But I don't like being seen in a swimming suit."

"Aw, c'mon. What's a little cellulite among friends?"

". . .I have scars."

"So? I have one from my appendectomy that's a humdinger. No one's perfect, Kris. People at the pool probably won't even notice—or care. And if they do, that's *their* problem. We have to be able to accept that things happen and realize that God allows them in order for us to grow and develop as mature believers. Knowing we are accepted by the Lord can sometimes help us to be able to accept our own human failings and imperfections. If He can accept us, we should learn how to, too."

Mandy had been rattling on, and Kristin wanted to reply, but found herself with such a tight throat that she couldn't form words when she felt the presence of an odd, aching voice that did seem to beg to be filled with deeper Christian growth. Meat was what Mandy offered, not just scriptural milk. Mandy was a young woman, but she had a Christian faith of true maturity, seasoned so deliciously with humor. Then Mandy glanced across and brought the heel of her hand to her forehead.

"There I go again. Maybe I'd better hobble over to that bench so I can sit down and get the required leverage to remove my foot from my mouth again. I didn't mean to preach at you."

Kristin managed a weak smile. "I was just mulling over what you said. You're not only a very amusing girl, but a truly wise woman in the wisdom of the Lord."

"I try. . . . Sincerely, Kristin, I didn't mean to hurt your feelings, or to trivialize something that is obviously of great concern to you. I've accepted that I'll never be perfect. I've learned to live with the fact. And I'd decided that I can like myself the way God made me and hope that others will too. If they don't like me, that's their problem. With Mandy Gentry, what you see is what you get. A committed Christian woman who tries her best but will sometimes fail."

"And what I've got," Kristin said, "is a real friend. I know that you didn't mean to hurt my feelings, Mandy. I'm probably too sensitive about how I look."

Mandy eyed her. "I think that perhaps you are," she agreed in a frank tone. "The scars carried in your memory are probably more easily detected than those on your skin."

"That's exactly what the surgeon told Aunt Delilah," Kristin admitted. "Maybe they do seem so glaringly visible to me because of my background. Once upon a time I used to be a model. . .I was groomed to be perfect. . .camouflaged to be flawless before the cameras."

For a moment, for perhaps the first time in her entire life, Mandy Gentry was found speechless.

"I remember you! No wonder you looked so familiar to me

when we met at the baggage carousel!" She gasped and gave a delighted little squeal of excitement. "Oh, Kristin, you were my all-time ideal. Your face and figure were everywhere, touting makeup, jeans, sportswear, cosmetics. You were my idol. Why, I even taped a picture of you modeling a bikini on our refrigerator to encourage me to stick with my diet the summer I lost ten pounds. Wow, Mom and Dad are going to be amazed when I go back to Kirkwood and tell them who I've been chumming around with!"

"Please don't tell anyone here," Kristin said. "It's odd, and while I've made a whole new life for myself in Southern Illinois and no one's remembered me as the girl I used to be, suddenly, now, it seems as if I'm forced to face and deal with a lot of old issues I'd rather not acknowledge."

"It's a promise," Mandy agreed.

"Thanks. Now, what do you say that we go get something to eat? As hungry as I am, when I leave this ranch I may end up going back to Camden Corners and taping Christy Brinkley's picture to my fridge to discourage me!" Kristin joked.

Laughing, feeling better, the girls joined the other guests for lunch, then trailed toward their quarters to let their meals digest before preparing to go for a swim.

"Want to come in?" Kristin invited as she fished for her room key.

"I may's well," Mandy decided. "Hey! Your phone light's blinking. You've got a message."

"I wonder what it could be?"

"There's one way to find out."

Kristin picked up the receiver and was connected with the desk. "There's a message for me?" she inquired.

"Hang on a minute," the desk worker requested. "I'll connect you."

"Ms. Allen? This is Dace Kendrick. I've been trying to contact you all morning. Thanks for returning my call."

*Dace Kendrick?*

The mention of his name sent her pulse thudding like the hoofbeats of a runaway horse.

"Oh. I. . .uh. . .you're welcome." *Now what does he want?*

"I'd like to see you, to apologize over last night."

"There's no need," Kristin said, hating how stiff and formal her voice sounded. "The flowers arrived. I've accepted your apology."

"Flowers can't begin to make up for the damage I've done."

*No they can't!* Kristin thought. *Nothing can!*

"I behaved in a a very unChristian manner last night," Dace went on, "that would not be tolerated from any of my employees. They'd have been dismissed immediately for accosting a guest in such a manner. I feel like a fool. So please, Ms. Allen, let me see you personally to apologize. I'll feel better and can hope to undo the shabby example I set for my help. . . ."

"I. . .isn't talking, now, good enough?" Kristin inquired. "It's quite acceptable to me."

"Our clash occurred in public, it seems suitable that an amicable apology should be a public statement, too. I was thinking more in terms of taking you out to dinner in Rapid City to try to make up for my insulting indiscretion."

"I. . .I really don't know about that," Kristin said.

Mandy, who was seated beside her on the satin covered bed, was fairly squirming, as she leaned close, listening.

"Tonight, at seven?" he suggested, but with the tone of one accustomed to issuing orders and having them obeyed. "Please—?"

"I'm touched, and appreciative, but I really—"

Kristin was not expecting it. Her grip on the receiver was loose, and in no time at all, Mandy had snatched it from her, and thrust out her left hand, clamping her finger over Kristin's surprised lips, so she could make only muffled protests.

"I'd really *love* to go, Mr. Kendrick," Mandy cooed in a

breathless voice, a passable imitation of Kristin's tone. "I'll be ready at seven. Sweet of you to ask me. Good-bye, now. See you tonight!"

Quickly she hung up before Kristin could react or wrest the phone back and wreck the evening's plans.

Dazed, sputtering with disbelief, Kristin stared at a blushing Mandy who couldn't even meet her stormy eyes.

"How on earth could you do this to me?" She hissed.

Mandy looked mortified. "I. . .I don't know. It's like something just came over me. I'll admit I'm impulsive, but not to the degree where I ever believed myself capable of being an imposter. Kristin, I'm sorry, but I'm also not sorry, if you can follow that. Something just came over me, and the way you were acting, I knew that you were going to turn him down. And, well, sometime's I'm impulsive. I don't always mind my own business, either."

"Mandy, you were positively brazen. Shameless! And you sounded almost exactly like me. Heaven knows what that man is going to think of me now."

"I really did sound like you, didn't I?" Mandy mused.

"Don't try to change the subject on me, Amanda Gentry!"

"Well, believe me, Kristin, if I could manage to *look* like you I'd gladly take your place tonight."

Kristin moaned at the thought. "I can't do it. I won't do it. I've got to get out of it. Call him back, Mandy, and give him my, your, *our* regrets. Quick! Right now—"

Mandy stared across the room and locked the fingers of both hands around her knees. She gave Kristin a bland smile in the face of her tall, dark-haired friend's distress.

"Among my many flaws is the fact that I'm a bit mulish, too. The answer is no, Kris. If you *really* want out of your date with Dace Kendrick tonight, you'll have to wriggle out of it on your own."

"Nice of you, since it was *you* who got me into it."

"If you really don't want to go, there's the phone."

Kristin stared at it, but did nothing.

Suddenly Mandy let out a whoop and tossed a pillow at Kristin. "You can't fool me, Kristi Allen, you *do* want to go."

"Yes, I suppose I do," Kristin said. "Bu. . .but only to find out a little bit about a man who once upon a time proposed to my sister."

"You really think that *she* is the infamous *her?*"

"Positive. If I'm wrong, I'll eat my hat." She tossed her Stetson toward the dresser. "And my boots, too. . . ." She jerked them off and clunked them to the floor. "Now let's get ready to go for a swim."

"A swim? Kristin, your date tonight changes everything. Won't you want all afternoon to get ready?"

"Mandy, you're forgetting who you're talking to. Why, I know makeup shortcuts that could have me ready ten minutes from now."

"Then let's go!" Mandy said. "I'll meet you outside in five minutes. But we won't swim very long because I'll have to come back and take a nap."

"A nap?" Kristin echoed, confused.

"Uh-huh, because I'm going to be staying up late so you can tell me about every romantic moment of your night alone with the big boss of the Circle K spread. . . ."

## four

"What time is it?" Kristin asked.

"Six-forty-five," Mandy replied and groaned with vicarious tension. "I'm going to have to go to my room soon. This is just like anticipating Christmas morning when you're a kid. I can't wait for Dacian to arrive. Aren't you excited?"

Kristin thought it over. "Nervous is more like it."

"Well, don't worry about how you look," Mandy said. "This afternoon was fun and the results were worth our combined efforts. You'll be turning heads tonight."

Kristin glanced at the full-length mirror on the closet door. Her shiny black hair hung loose, full, and free, just caressing her shoulders that were glowing for the afternoon sun's searing kiss. Her makeup, suitable for an evening out, made her features seem intense, vibrant, even mysterious, Mandy concluded.

Kristin's dress of tangerine crepe looked as if it had been made for her. It had a full, flowing skirt, nipped-in waist, and fitted low scooped bodice with dainty spaghetti straps. A heartshaped gold pendant on a delicate chain, with a sizeable diamond in the center, perfectly accentuated the neckline and rested just above the hint of cleavage.

A year before Kristin had bought the dress on impulse when she'd gone shopping at the Honey Creek Mall in Terre Haute, Indiana, but she'd never worn it.

When she tried it on for Mandy's reaction, the round-faced girl had almost swooned.

Kristin had studied her reflection. "I can't wear it. . . ."

"Why not?"

"Because. . .just because. It shows a scar. . . ."

Mandy's lips folded into a firm line and she touched her fingertip to the bottle of liquid makeup on the vanity table top. She dabbed it to the tiny, white, dimpled scar on Kristin's shoulder and it disappeared as if it had never existed.

"Wear it!" Mandy ordered in a no-nonsense tone.

Now an hour later Mandy was monitoring the time. "Six-fifty and counting," she announced.

Kristin shivered and goose bumps rippled across her tawny flesh. Mandy noticed, but misunderstood.

"It may get cool tonight, Kris. I have just the exact little cover-up for you to take along. It's a white, lacy shawl with a dainty fringed border. You can secure it with a loose knot. It'll be perfect."

Mandy darted into her room and then rejoined Kristin a moment later, illustrating how the wrap would work effectively.

"You're a dear," Kristin said.

"I've got to go now," Mandy replied and gave Kristin an impulsive hug and an affectionate kiss on the cheek. "He's going to be here any moment. So forget about what happened last night and let this be a new beginning. Incidentally, if Dacian Kendrick wants to keep you out late, stay. You don't have to come home by eleven o'clock to tell me all about it." Mandy gave a good-natured shrug. "I'm going to be seeing Billy Joe tonight. And there's always tomorrow. . . ."

Dace arrived promptly at seven. When Kristin saw his white Corvette pull up in front of her quarters, she was torn between excitement and dismay, and seesawed with sensations of eagerness about the evening and an almost overwhelming desire to ignore his knock and hide out for the night.

But she knew that Mandy Gentry would never let her get away with it. Kristin almost laughed when she pictured Mandy next door, peeking from behind the curtain of her darkened room, moaning to herself, "This is heaven. I'm in love!"

When Kristin opened the door to Dacian's knock, for a

moment she wondered if that was the emotion that swept over her.

She felt the pulse at her neck throb, probably visible to Dacian, like a butterfly's fluttering wing, as she felt almost overpowered by his appeal. At that moment, his snapshot would've made the perfect inclusion in Webster's Dictionary to illustrate the definition of "handsome."

He was wearing a crisp beige linen summer suit that perfectly accentuated his lean, muscular build and his burnished tan from being outdoors so much. His hair was casually styled, but she knew such grooming did not come inexpensively. His cologne made her feel almost dizzy when she inhaled deeply. And his blue eyes, that had been sparking forked lightning the night before, a barometer that registered the intensity of his anger, were now as calm and open as the cloudless South Dakota sky.

"Dacian Kendrick," he spoke, when Kristin found herself unable. He extended his hand. "You're Kristin Allen?"

"Yes."

He gave a polite, deferential nod. "I'm pleased to meet you. Welcome to the Kendrick Circle K Ranch."

Krista gave a nervous smile. "Thank you. You sound about to give a testimonial to all that the dude ranch offers," she blurted nervously, to fill the stifling silence.

Dacian laughed. "Sorry. I was only trying to start fresh with you, Kristin, in the manner I should've greeted you last night."

"Oh."

He paused, then looked hesitant. "Can we begin again? Please? I don't know what came over me last night. It's bothered me all day. . . ."

Kristin was touched by his uncertainty. "I think that's the nicest suggestion I've heard all day. Dacian Kendrick, I'm very pleased to make your acquaintance, and I'm sure I'll enjoy my stay here."

"Now you're starting to sound like a travel brochure," he

teased. "Since you already know what the Circle K has to offer, let's head for Rapid City. There's plenty to see and do, and I've got what I think will be a memorable night planned for us."

Kristin's heart gave a sudden lurch when he helped her into his Corvette, and when he was circling around to the driver's side, she sneaked a wave in Mandy's direction.

She realized that no matter where they went, or what they did, it would be a truly momentous occasion.

When Kristin's parents were still alive, she'd been deemed too young to date. After finding herself in Aunt Dee's care, she'd been too shy. Eventually, she knew that boys considered her unapproachable. She'd been kissed a few times while she was in high school. And she had gone to the roller rink on group outings. But then such adventures became off limits for a well-paid girl who couldn't afford black and blue marks from falling. So she'd never really had a *bona fide* date.

Until tonight. . . .

Dace Kendrick had invited her out because he wanted to make amends. But Kristin was intent on enjoying her first date as if he'd requested her company because he considered her the most beautiful, fascinating woman in the world.

And that's what she tried to be as he drove them toward Rapid City. She listened to him, marveling at the melodious tone of his voice as he explained how the nearby Badlands, considered some of the most beautiful and rugged country in the world, had been formed. He explained about what his ancestors had faced when they'd crossed South Dakota's plains, intent on going further west, how they had confronted the Badlands, turned back in despair, but then carved out a rich and rewarding life.

At the fancy restaurant they were shown to the table Dacian had reserved for them. The meal progressed flawlessly, and the evening was as perfect as the previous night's confrontation had been ugly.

Over coffee, Dace regarded Kristin by candlelight as the conversation flowed.

Dacian asked about her, and she told him about her Roving Maid business, the people she worked for, but was carefully evasive about anything that could link her to Janice.

When he asked a direct question about her family, she said only that her immediate family was very small, and then she deftly turned the tables by inquiring about his family. He regaled her with fascinating trivia about the close-knit, very accomplished Kendrick clan for most of the meal.

Kristin felt a ripple of pleasure when she realized that Dace was truly enjoying her company, and knowing that he did made her own experience more fulfilling.

As the evening progressed she felt her breath quicken when he looked at her across the table and she was trying to fathom the inexplicable expression in his eyes.

Amusement?

Admiration?

Affection?

A touch of perplexity?

Eventually he stared at her until she felt a flush spread upwards from her cheeks, and the heat disappeared into her hairline.

"A penny for your thoughts, Dace."

"I was just thinking that I can't believe I made such an utter fool of myself last night. Not only was it a stupid mistake, but I must've been blinded by disgust not to see at a glance that you weren't who I thought you were."

"Oh," Kristin said, and took a sip of her coffee, then toyed with her after dinner mint as she wished she'd left well enough alone and not accidentally turned their talk toward the very topic she'd wanted to avoid.

"At a glance you seemed almost a dead ringer for her, that woman," he went on to explain, "but on closer inspection that's where the resemblance ends. She had a hard beauty. And she was somewhat older, too. Your looks are fresh, simple. . .vulnerable. . . pure. If I'd looked at you closely last night, I'd have seen the difference."

"You were upset," Kristin dismissed the incident.

"The understatement of the year, Kristin, but when I thought you had the audacity to return to the Circle K after what you had done last year, I became so infuriated that I couldn't see straight."

"It wasn't *me* who did that. It was *her!*" Kristin defended to Dacian just as Mandy had pointed out the same logic to her that very morning, when it seemed as if the line between sisterhood and self had failed to exist to the others.

"Forgive me," he said. "I know that. It's just so uncanny to be sitting across from you, as if I were facing a younger, prettier version of *her.* I suppose that I still find it disconcerting and difficult to take in, although, last night if I hadn't been so unhinged, I'd have known that you were not her, Kristin. But I wasn't listening to what you were saying any more than I was listening to how you said it. She had an affected, high society accent. And you sound like. . .a real person."

"I know," Kirstin said in a resigned tone.

Janice's la-di-da accent had been one of the first things she'd undertaken to learn when she'd been tucked under Aunt Dee's wing and moved to New York City.

Suddenly Kristin realized what she'd admitted.

"I. . .I mean, I know what those people are like. So often phonies," she quickly clarified.

Dace regarded her a long moment, seemed about to speak further, then looked as if he'd decided against it.

"Last night I committed one terrible indiscretion, and here I am tonight, blundering into another by talking of the other woman to the lady of the moment. I'm sorry. Just let me add that I had no excuse to light into you and take you to task like I did, and I wouldn't have except out of family loyalty and misguided anger. The resemblance is such that you could be that woman's little sister. . . ."

Silence spun out, intense, upsetting, and Kristin's mind swirled as she tried to think of something to say, other than what was on the tip of her tongue: an admission that the infamous other woman had looked like Kristin's older sister because she *was!*

"Everyone gets told that she or he resembles someone else at one time or another, I'm sure," Kristin replied in an offhand manner. "I'm sorry that you were hurt as you were."

"It's over now," Dace said. "And from the experience I learned a few things about myself. . .and how to deal with women. Especially devious, dishonest, calculating Jezebels."

Then Dace fell silent and she knew that he was thinking about what had been, what might have been, and what was now. It was poignantly clear that he'd opened up his life and let himself become vulnerable, and placed his love and deep feelings in the care of a heartless woman who had no compassion nor consideration. The set to his lips seemed to warn the world of women that he wouldn't be caught off guard like that again.

"It's late," Dace said as he assisted Kristin from her chair, left a tip, took care of the tab, and escorted her toward his car.

It was a gorgeous night, with a sky like purple velvet, spangled with stars, the perfect background for the full, golden moon. Impulsively Dace took Kristin's hand, and they strolled along, hands swinging. Suddenly Kristin began to laugh.

"What's so amusing?"

"I haven't walked along like this," she said, squeezing his hand, lifting it to gesture what she meant, "since kindergarten, what seems like a century ago."

"As children we resented having to do what we didn't know we'd enjoy as adults," he grinned.

"I hadn't thought of it like that," Kristin said. "I always

seemed to get paired with some grubby-handed little boy."

Dacian stopped. He regarded her as her face was bathed in the moon's silvery glow.

"And did any of those grubby-handed little boys grow up to become handsome men? Who'd like to marry you. . .and father grubby-handed little boys who'd grow up to become handsome men?" He asked as if suddenly he found it terribly important to know.

"I'm afraid not."

"Then there's no one in particular?" he asked, his tone careful. "No one waiting for you back home in Illinois?"

The question that would've been embarrassing to answer truthfully to some people, was one that she was glad she could give Dacian Kendrick.

"No. . .there's no one."

He brushed a kiss across her cheek, then began walking, swinging her hand, grinning, as if the assurance had been as pleasant for him to receive as it had been for Kristin to give.

"I'm glad," he said. "Very, very happy. You're so young, you probably don't understand the feelings of a man my age. A man who's had to accept the yoke of responsibility when not much more than a boy and live accordingly. Sometimes denying himself the simple things that others take for—" Abruptly he clipped off further words.

"When your father died," Kristin said, remembering information from his lashing out from the night before.

"Yes. At age sixteen, as the oldest son, I had to accept the fact that I had to keep the family together, work so that we could prosper and be secure. Then later on I had to keep in mind that it wasn't only the Kendrick family's fate that relied on my efforts, but the security of the people in my employ, who turned to me, trusted in me. Those are things someone as young as you probably hasn't had to face, if you're fortunate and life's been kind to you."

"Believe me, I've had my moments of trial," Kristin said. "I'm twenty-three. You're not that much older, Dacian."

"Thirty," he replied. "And that's old enough so that I have the urge to—"

Dacian shook his head in apparent confusion of thought or feeling, sighed, and then fell silent.

"Urge to what?" Kristin prompted as he unlocked the Corvette.

"Nothing," he said. "It's not important."

"The way you sighed, I think whatever you feel, or dream, is very important to you."

"Maybe," he said, and gave her hand another squeeze, then leaned toward her, and as the South Dakota breeze blew a wing of hair away from her smooth cheek, he deposited a tender kiss there. "And perhaps sometime I'll tell you all about it. . . ."

Without being told, she sensed that he wanted to find a woman, settle down, and stop being all things to all people so that he could be himself with the woman he loved and the children they would have to carry on a fine Kendrick family tradition in the land that they loved.

All the things, in a slightly different form, that she, too, had dreamed about during the dark lonely nights, wanting them for her own, but fearing she would never possess them.

Kristin's heart squeezed with a painful pang like a stab.

What a fool her sister had been. . .to turn down a man like this. . .scarring him so cruelly in the process that she shaped how he now dealt with all other women. But how lucky Dace had been to escape Janice, delivered from her deceits in time.

And how Dacian Kendrick would hate her, Kris feared, if he knew who she really was. . . .

"Earlier this evening you mentioned a housekeeper," Kristin remarked. "And I sensed you weren't referring to someone on the Circle K's housekeeping staff. Don't you live at the ranch?"

"Uh-uh. I have quarters there if I want to stay, but just as an executive leaves the corporate office and goes home for the night, so do I need to leave the Circle K and get away, too." He gave her a long look, then laid his hand over hers. "But something tells me that for the duration of your stay, I may be staying at the Circle K almost 'round the clock. I have a residence on private property, acreage that adjoins the family concerns." He paused. "Maybe I'll take you there some time so you can see my ranch."

"I'd like that," Kristin murmured.

Dace didn't respond, and when she said no more he seemed not to notice. Perhaps he, like she, was thinking of the other woman, Kristin's look-alike, who had probably gone there with him before, with him believing she wanted to share his dreams. Had there been others, too? Was he a womanizer as Jan had hinted all cowboys on dude ranches tended to be? Was Dacian being attentive because it was a good business tactic to romance a guest for the duration of her stay? For the gain of subsequent back-home word-of-mouth free advertising?

Kristin realized with sudden impact that she didn't want to know. Janice had warned her about dude ranch romances. And Mandy had passed judgment that cruise ship romances certainly didn't last.

Was she a fool to believe that she had a future with this remarkable man, when she knew, as he didn't, that the past was waiting in the wings to cause devastation in the present and prevent even the idea of a future?

She knew that all the women eyed the big boss of the Circle K with interest. Surely he wasn't immune. And certainly he frequently looked back with equal fascination. . . .

Kristin found herself feeling insecure and wondering exactly what were Dace's motives. Had he wined and dined her as a public relations maneuver after destructive business behavior the night before? Or had he used it as an excuse to ask her out? So that he could set the scene for a seduction and romance her, substituting a look-alike girlfriend for a woman he despised. . .but perhaps still desired?

She would rather never know what it was to feel such longing and desire for a man. . .than to know that he was *using her as a reflection of love.*

Kristin was more confused than ever when Dace stopped in front of her quarters.

"You're quiet," he observed.

"I was just thinking."

"About what?"

Kristin gave a light laugh. "That's for me to know and you to find out."

"Ah, then, I will," he said. "Because nothing happens on the Circle K Ranch that I don't eventually find out about it."

Although it was spoken as light banter, the warning went straight to Kristin's heart, filling her with dread, as she considered the secret that she, and Mandy, kept.

"It's late. Time for me to go in," she whispered, suddenly desperate to escape his compelling presence.

"I'll see you to your door," he said.

"We'll be quiet," she murmured, "so we don't disturb my neighbors."

He squeezed her hand in silent acceptance.

"Kristin, thank you," Dace said in a solemn tone. "It's been nice."

"You're welcome," she replied. "I enjoyed it too."

"There will be other nights."

At the promise, her heart leaped, until she reminded herself that it was probably just words, a patly-phrased parting promise that actually meant nothing.

"I. . .I'd like that."

"Then starting tomorrow night, if you're agreeable? For the hayride?"

Her heart suddenly soared. All of her misgivings had been in vain!

"Sounds like fun," Kristin said, unable to believe what was

happening. Then insecure specters moved into the shadows of her mind. "But is that a wise business move?" She tested him.

"Business move?" He echoed, frowning down at her. "Whatever are you talking about?"

"I think that half of the women at the Circle K are in love with you," Kristin said. "Wouldn't it make more sense to circulate among them all? Keep your guests happy and hopeful?"

Dacian gave a ragged laugh.

"In matters of money, yes. Matters of the heart, no. I've already given so much of myself to the family business, Kristin. It's time that I set about the business of. . .someday having my own family."

Suddenly, as Dace looked into Kristin's eyes, she felt a weak sensation slide through her, leaving her feeling as if she might collapse beneath the weight of the knowledge that Dacian Kendrick was looking at her as if she might be the woman he had been waiting for.

It couldn't be.

She wouldn't let it be.

She couldn't let it be.

For she would not be able to bear it if he ever again looked at her with the threatening hatred that had been in his eyes only twenty-four hours before.

The realization made her feel boneless. Her respiration was thready and insufficient, leaving her feeling short of breath and oxygen starved.

She wasn't sure if she felt dizzy and swayed, or if Dace pulled her into his arms. But suddenly he was embracing her, dropping kisses to her hair, her temples, her cheeks, then his lips sought her mouth and he kissed her with an intensity that she knew she would never forget.

It was as if he were trying to brand her as his, while driving from his tortured mind memories of a woman he'd once wanted by creating equally as heady moments with a woman who looked just like *her* but was her opposite in every other way.

"It's time for you to go in," he said, his voice husky and thick with emotion. "Before I beg you to stay."

"Good night, Dace," Kristin whispered.

"Stay sweet," he ordered.

And then he was gone.

Kristin let herself into her room. She closed the door and collapsed against it, still feeling weak and breathless, but this time from the thrilling forcefulness of Dacian's kisses, not her nervous tension.

She half-expected Mandy to knock on her door and come dancing into her quarters, gasping, "Dacian kissed you! I saw it! The most handsome man in South Dakota kissed you!"

But when Mandy failed to materialize, Kristin realized that either her new friend was fast asleep, or she was out with Billy Joe making a few unforgettable memories of her own.

Kristin thought of the person, the other woman, who had given Dacian Kendrick some unforgettable memories he'd sooner not remember, and she glanced at her watch, wondering if it was too late to call Janice.

Then she thought of the kind of hours Janice kept: first as a rich wife whose sole occupation was "shopping 'til dropping," and then as a wealthy divorcee who could sleep until noon and party until the wee hours as she sifted through likely prospects to find her next husband. Kristin decided it wasn't likely her big sister was tucked in for the night.

Although she didn't want to talk to Janice on one hand, and have her pleasant evening tarnished by condescension, criticism, or cynicism, she knew that she had to put her worries to rest, or else clearly define the problem she faced.

"It would be a dream come true to find out that she has never even heard of Dacian Kendrick," Kristin whispered to herself after she reached the switchboard and put through a long distance call to her sister.

Jan didn't pick up the receiver until the third ring, and she answered in such a tone of voice that Kristin realized that it *was* a wonder Dace hadn't realized his error as soon as Kristin had opened her mouth.

"Hi, Jan? This is Kristin."

"Darling, I got your message—"

"I thought perhaps I'd have better luck catching you tonight."

"I just got in moments ago. You know how it is in New York City: busy, busy. And how are things in the Wild West?"

"I'm having a good time," Kristin said.

"With the sweaty horses, stinging insects, grubby children, scorching sun—"

"I've hardly noticed for all of the romantic men," Kristin interrupted.

"You've been behaving yourself?" Janice asked and gave a naughty sounding giggle.

"Probably better than you have," Kristin retorted.

*"Touche!"* Jan said in a droll tone. "So you've discovered some handsome, *macho* cowboys have you?"

"Um-hm, although I just arrived yesterday, I went out this evening with a cowboy who has a brand new Corvette."

Jan gave a little croon of approval. "He's rich?"

"Very."

"Handsome?"

"Exceptionally so."

"Intelligent?"

"Top of his college class."

"Ambitious?"

"He runs the family business."

"Kristin, darling, are you *finally* coming to your senses? Aunt Dee will be so happy to hear that you're not only finally dating but keeping company with a man who has solid prospects."

"He seems very nice. A little bit impulsive. And he has something of a temper when he's driven to it. But I really like him."

"And does this Mr. Perfect have a name?" Janice inquired. "So that we'll have something to call him? I know Dee will want to know."

"An unusual name," Kristin said and gave a little yawn. "Dace." She prayed that Janice would gloss over the fact without a bit of alarm and go on to her next question.

But when Kristin's answer earned a startled gasp, her hopes plummeted and she knew that there wasn't going to be a reprieve.

*"Dacian Kendricks?!"* Janice cried, her refined accent forgotten. "Oh, Kristin, how *could* you? How could you be so foolish as to get involved with *him?"*

Kristin feigned innocence. "Simple. We met. He asked me out. I accepted. And we just spent a wonderful evening together."

Janice muttered an oath. "Oh Kristin—"

"Jan, what's wrong? You seem so upset. Do you know him?"

"It's *him*," Janice said. "The cowboy who wanted me to marry him. The one I turned down. I should have warned you about him, but I didn't think you were going to the same dude ranch Cissy and I went to. The man was a beast when I broke it off with him. He vividly painted a romantic little hearts and flowers picture of our future together, and I tried to play the part for awhile, but realized there were easier ways to earn a place in society and a right to a man's bank account, without putting up with all Dace would've dished out. I tried, but deep down I just couldn't buy what he was trying to sell me on—"

Kristin wanted to close her ears as her sister railed on, spilling every ugly detail. She pinched her eyes shut, leaned her forehead against the cool wall, and she began to understand perfectly why Dacian despised her sister the way he did.

He'd offered Janice his love.

But she settled for nothing less than cutting out his heart, slashing his private dreams to ribbons.

"You'd better watch out for him," Janice repeated the warning in a grim tone. "You were right when you said that he's intelligent. He's smart enough to benefit from long-range planning. Why. . .he probably knows just who you are. . .and he's romancing you so that he can get back at me. Believe me, Krissie, when it comes to that forsaken ranch of his, nothing goes on that he doesn't know about it. Why, if a leaf turns over in the corral, he's aware of it. And he's just the hypocritical type who'd find this tawdry, tacky little debacle amusing. But if that's what Dace's doing, then he doesn't know me well enough to realize that such juvenile behavior won't bother me a'tall." She gave a careless sniff. "Let him play his childish games. Such behavior would never win me back. . . ."

Kristin realized that Janice was talking only about herself, and seemed not to notice or care if Kristin was wounded along the way.

"As smitten with me as Dacian was, I knew that he wasn't going to get over me fast. Such a. . .passionate man. But impulsive. And he has such a strange sense of loyalty and such an odd set of what he considered 'Christian ethics,' that I'll bet a block of Blue Chip stock that he's still carrying a torch for me! And if *that's* the case, then you're in even worse trouble than if he's got his heart set on revenge, Krissie, because no girl wants to settle for being a substitute for the real thing. Making do with her big sister's hand-me-down love."

Kristin felt near tears.

"Bu. . .but I like him," she protested softly, even as she hated herself for making the admission to a woman who obviously didn't know what it was to enter a relationship without balancing it out in dollars and cents, and realizing that a person couldn't attach a price tag to the human heart.

"Of course you like him, dear, because Dace is very good at what he does. He makes every woman between eight and eighty who comes to his ranch feel like the only girl in the world.

Why, he gobbles up pretty girls the way I can go through chocolates when I'm depressed. . . . Trust me, darling, you are no
match for him. Continue this mad affair, Krissie, and you'll
regret your folly. I really hate to ruin your dreams by giving
you this down-to-earth advice. But that's what big sisters are
for."

"Have you heard from Aunt Delilah?" Kristin changed the
subject.

"As a matter of fact, I did. She and Uncle Benchley will be
departing Heathrow a week from tomorrow. I'll have a limo
meet them at LaGuardia. She told me to give you her love.
And we'll be in touch when they arrive, so you and Dee can
have a little chitchat."

"All right."

"And I'm not going to tell Aunt Dee that you're mixed up
with Dacian, Kristin, and I would suggest that you don't
either. She'd be so worried. She *knew* what I went through last
year at this time."

"Well, it's late, and I've really got to go," Kristin said.

"Great talking to you, Krissie. Call again. And remember
what I said: Dacian isn't interested in you because of the kind
of girl you are, but because of *who* you are. His motives are
definitely suspect. Either revenge. Or trying to mold my
look-alike little sister into the sophisticated woman of his
dreams so he can enjoy a make-do love affair with a facsimile
of his old flame."

Kristin hung up without even saying good-bye, although
Janice was too involved in her cooing, kissy noise good-byes
to notice.

Kristin took a deep breath and tried to hold in the tears, but
they erupted with the force of a sneeze and a painful sob tore
from her throat.

She threw herself down on the bed and cried into her pillow
as she realized that her big sister, who liked to think that she

was so sophisticated and wise, might just be right about Dacian Kendrick. Perhaps they really were two of a kind.

Kristin had known Dace for only slightly more than twenty-four hours. Janice had been involved with him long enough for him to propose marriage.

Was Dacian toying with her?

Kristin thought back over their night together. The way he had said that Kristin looked so much like the other woman, did he know it for a fact? Was he testing Kristin to see if she would confess to the truth? Did he want to see if she would lie to him the way her sister had? And had he warned her that she would not get away with it? Janice had told her that nothing happened on the Circle K ranch without Dacian knowing about it. That fact wasn't news to her, for the same information had fallen from Dace's lips that very night.

Was he setting her up for an elaborate scheme? Despising her sister to the point that he didn't care who he hurt, so long as he could wreak his sick revenge?

Kristin realized she still did not really know if he liked her or loathed her.

And if Dacian Kendrick was truly as farsighted and long-reaching as Janice had insisted, Kristin realized that she would have no idea exactly where she stood with him until Dacian Kendrick decided to make the issue perfectly clear.

Then it dawned on her that even if he did like her, it was only a temporary stay from heartbreak and humiliation.

For she couldn't continue on forever keeping it a secret that her only sister was the woman who had spurned Dacian Kendrick and taught him the bitter tenets of faithless, untrue, unreturned love.

## five

It had been hours before Kristin fell asleep as her mind swirled with the possibilities surrounding her new and chaotic relationship with Dacian Kendrick.

Not long before dawn she drifted asleep, exhausted from crying, too weary to think.

Hours later there came a pounding upon her door.

Kristin sat up, blinked, looked around her, dazed and disoriented, startled to not be in her own bed in Camden Corners.

Then she remembered where she was.

And why.

Her caller knocked a little louder.

"Just a minute," Kristin called out.

She ran her fingers through her sleep-tangled hair, retrieved her robe from the chair beside the bed, scuffed into slippers and crossed the room, looking out the peephole before she undid the assortment of security devices.

A smiling Mandy was dressed and raring to go.

"Good morning, Sleepyhead!" She said in a bright tone.

"Hi. I guess I overslept." Kristin gestured at herself and the rumpled bed.

"If you hurry we can still make breakfast. Pancakes, sausage, and warm, buttery syrup appeals to me this morning."

"It does sound good," Kristin agreed and offered a wan smile as she collected clothing and toiletries, trying to keep her back and profile to her friend.

"You've been crying!" Mandy murmured in a shocked gasp.

She was across the room and tugged Kristin's shoulder, turning her so that they were face-to-face.

"You *have* been crying."

"I. . .I know," Kristin admitted in a quaking voice and squeezed her eyes shut for a moment, hoping to hold back more tears that prickled at her red swollen eyes.

"The night was that bad?" Mandy said. "That's too bad. I would've been in for details last night, except I was out with Billy Joe until so late I thought it wasn't appropriate to disturb you. But maybe I should've. It looks like you could've used a shoulder to cry on. He was a regular beast, huh?"

"No, actually, Dacian Kendrick couldn't have been more charming," Kristin said.

"What?" Mandy cried, perplexed, as her eyes were telling her one thing and her ears were hearing quite another.

"I had a wonderful time, Mandy. It was perhaps one of the . . .the. . .the. . .most wonderful nights of my entire life."

"Then why are you crying, pray tell?" Mandy asked.

"Because I don't know why Dacian was so nice to me."

"Because he likes you, silly. And you're more than just a little nice to look at, you know. Last night you looked like any man's daydream come true. Oh, and I also suppose you think that he's just being nice in order to fully apologize for his rotten behavior from the night before. But I saw the look on his face when he came to get you. I think apologizing was secondary, Kris. Definitely secondary."

"Dace Kendrick is an intelligent man, shrewd, long-reaching, farsighted—"

"Who am I talking to this morning?" Mandy asked. "It doesn't sound like the girl I know. I feel as if I'm being lectured by some unpleasant stranger."

"Sorry."

"Just what's gotten into you?"

Kristin sighed. "Maybe it's a case of who's gotten through to me."

"Okay. I give. Who?"

"I talked to Janice after I came in last night."

"You didn't! Oh, Kris, *why*? She sounds like nothing but a bucket of bad news."

"Why? Because the way I felt last night. . .I had to know if Janice really was the other woman. Maybe it was foolish, but I entertained hope against hope that she wasn't. Mandy, I feel about Dacian the way I have never felt about a man before. We got along so well last night, had such fun, that I felt as if he considered me the most wonderful woman in the world."

"Your head was swimming," Mandy empathized.

"Yes."

"And then you started dreaming."

Kristin nodded, then sighed again. "Until I woke up and realized what a nightmare it would be if Janice was Dacian's unrequited love. I wanted to know where I stood, Mandy. If Janice had never heard of Dacian, then I'd know that I could risk getting involved with Dace and not fear there being a secret between us."

"And a secret with the capacity to blow your worlds apart," Mandy said, understanding Kristin's inner fears.

"So I called Janice last night. You should've heard her," Kristin said, and she looked ill as she recalled. "She painted a totally different picture of Dacian than the impression he had given me."

"I'm not sure I should ask, and I'd probably be happier not knowing, but what did she tell you?"

"For starters. . .that Dacian was so smitten by her that she doubts that he ever got over her. She feels that he's still carrying a torch for her."

Mandy made a face. "Oh, give me a break. She sounds like she has an ego as big as the outdoors. She couldn't face herself in the mirror in the morning if she thought that he wasn't beating his breast, wearing sackcloth, and pouring ashes over his head on her behalf."

Kristin gave a weak laugh in spite of herself and her worries.

"I'm a glutton for punishment," Mandy said. "Tell me more."

"Well, she also says that he's vengeful. She believes that there's a good chance he knows exactly who I am, and that he's stringing me along, being the attentive, affectionate, considerate suitor so that he can make me fall in love with him, and then dump me, so that by hurting me he'll somehow get back at her."

"Stuff and nonsense! Pure egotism. And convoluted reasoning." Mandy gestured impatiently. "Go on, go on, surely it gets worse."

Kristin frowned reflectively. "No, basically that's it. Although she expounded on the topics at great length, telling me what she thinks about Dace." Kristin's voice shook. "Excuse me," she said quickly, "while I run in and take a shower."

*And have another good cry.*

Kristin exited the bathroom ten minutes later, dressed, and toweling her hair.

A definitely nettled Mandy sat with her arms folded over her ample chest.

"You've told me what your sister thinks of Dace. I have a hunch I know how *you* really feel about him, or you wouldn't have cried the night away. Would you like me to tell you what others think about Dacian Kendrick?"

"If you feel compelled to. I don't know if it will make any difference. I feel so confused. . .I wish we'd never met. To think I came here to have fun."

"And you will have it. *With* Dace."

"He did ask to accompany me on the hayride tonight."

"See? Great!" Mandy's expression brightened. "Billy Joe's my date. And, speaking of Billy Joe, he's the source I'm quoting. Last night I asked him about Dace, and he told me about all there was to tell. Listening to him, seeing the expression on his face, I can't believe that Dace is a petty, vengeful, grudge-bearing man. Not someone who loves kids the way he does."

"He's been very good to his brothers and sisters," Kristin agreed. "He told me about them last night. And I know it wasn't an act, like Jan hinted his family loyalty might be."

"If it were an act, kid, he'd have a hard time maintaining it, year in, year out, for two weeks each summer. Especially when you consider that it's costing him dear."

"What are you talking about?"

"The fact that every year, for two weeks of the summer, Dace Kendrick turns down paying guests because he reserves the entire ranch for kids' enjoyment. Not just any kids, *sick children*."

"Mandy, I had no idea. . . ."

"Most of the guests don't know. But the staff, of course, is aware."

Quickly Mandy sketched in the background.

When they were youngsters, Dace Kendrick's older brother had died of leukemia. At the time the Kendricks were not wealthy, there were bills to pay, other children to care for, and the burden of a serious illness had taken a toll on the family's emotional and financial resources.

"An anonymous person knew that Dace's older brother had always dreamed of going to Disneyland. It was a trip beyond the Kendrick family's ability to finance, and this unknown benefactor donated money sufficient not only to take the dying boy to Disneyland, but to send along his family as well."

Mandy was getting misty-eyed, and Kristin suddenly felt that way, too.

"That dream vacation for a sick little boy and his family gave them lasting memories of good times to offset the effects of living daily with inevitable tragedy."

"He's been through a lot," Kristin murmured.

"And that's what makes him such a tough, strong, enduring man, with a compassionate Christian nature to soften the rough edges from his human nature.

"According to Billy Joe Blaylock, Dace, even as a child, had been deeply affected by his brother's illness. He knew what the stranger's generosity had meant to others, and when he was scarcely more than a child himself, he vowed to someday do for other children and their families what was done for the Kendricks.

"He does have a good side," Kristin acknowledged.

"And his word given is a vow that goes unbroken," Mandy said. "Every summer at least one hundred seriously ill children, who are in remission or are well enough to come here, spend a two-week vacation on a real ranch. All expenses paid."

"They must look forward to it months before they get to go," Kristin said.

"And talk about it for months afterwards," Mandy added. "When I was a kid I can remember the lure horses, rodeos, and ranches held for me. Well, your Dacian Kendrick, my dear, makes dreams happen for a lot of children and their families, and it's been going on for years and years. The Operation: Recovery Rodeo is a tradition in these parts and draws major rodeo riders from all over the United States, who particpate and donate their purses to support various childrens' hospitals nationwide."

"He's hardly 'my Dacian Kendrick,'" Kristin clarified.

"I think he could be," Mandy said. She paused. "And so does Billy Joe Blaylock."

"You've discussed this with Billy Joe?" Kristin cried, embarrassed.

"Actually, no. He asked me about you. So I told him I'd tell him what there was to know about you if he'd respond to my questions about Dace. It seemed a fair swap. And I didn't tell him about your sister, although he's no fan of the infamous

Janice, either."

Kristin, who had felt her almost obsessive desire for the protection of privacy slip in the past days, felt suddenly vulnerable.

"I'm not sure I approve of the deal you two struck."

"Billy Joe wants for Dace the same thing that I want for you, Kris, happiness. And we happen to think that you two could find it in each other."

"If it weren't for Janice."

"Do you really think it will, would, make that much difference to Dace if, or when, he finds out?"

"I don't know," Kristin said. "Maybe Billy Joe could tell you, but don't you dare ask him, because I certainly don't have a clue."

"You will after tonight when you go on a hayride and are snuggled on a wagon load of soft, clean straw, beneath a golden moon, with stars twinkling overhead, and—" Mandy broke off her litany of details and leaped to her feet. "So let's get started with our day, concentrate on happy thoughts and positive thinking, and prepare for us both to have the night of our lives this evening."

"Sounds good," said Kristin, who suddenly felt so much better. She cinched her western belt and smoothed her designer jeans over her trim hips. "Mess hall cooks—here we come!"

ᴓ

After breakfast the girls went for a ride. The cowboy in charge of the corral stock gave Mandy a different mount, also gentle, and placed her and the horse in Kristin's more experienced care.

"But I like Molly," Mandy protested.

"Sorry," the cowboy said and gave an amused grin. "She's an ol' pet, and everyone loves Molly, but we keep her up at the corral unless we run short of stock and then we'll only let an experienced rider take her out. You see, the old girl has this bad habit of getting out, becoming a bit headstrong, and heading for home at the neighboring spread where she lives for eleven months out of the year."

"Oh, okay," Mandy said, laughing, and settled for Waco, a sorrel quarterhorse gelding.

Following the girls' ride, they watched a tennis match, went for lunch, took a swim, and then sunned themselves beside the pool as they talked about plans for the night.

"It'll be fun," Mandy assured.

"I hope so," Kristin said.

"Don't worry. I know so."

Kristin was not as confident as Mandy was. Each time they neared the headquarters that day she'd glanced to the slot where Dace parked his Corvette. The private parking area was mockingly empty, causing her heart to sink anew each time her searching glance was not rewarded with the presence of his car.

"We probably ought to go to our rooms and think about getting ready for dinner tonight," Mandy said, yawning from the exertion of an hour in the pool combined with the cloying heat.

"You're right," Kristin said and immediately arose, collecting her beach jacket, her leather sandles, her sunglasses, floppy hat, and sunscreen lotion.

A lethargic Mandy was slower gathering her gear.

Kristin walked a few steps ahead of her, hoping that she didn't seem impatient in her desire to cast a quick glance in the direction of Dace's parking slot. Surely as late as it was and with his plans to take her to the hayride, he would have returned to the ranch while she lazed away the afternoon by the pool.

When she saw his parking slot was still empty, she felt drenched with disappointment, and it was an effort to muster passable enthusiasm to respond to Mandy's excited predictions for the hayride.

"See to it that you and Dace sit near Billy Joe and me," she ordered. "We're all going to have such fun together."

"Okay. I promise," Kristin said. "Want to come into my room for a little while? I'll get a soda from the machine and we can split it."

"Sounds great," Mandy said. "I'm parched."

Kristin unlocked the door to her quarters. The telephone on the stand beside her bed blinked a steady rhythm

"I'll get the soda," Mandy offered, digging in the pocket of her beach robe where coins jingled. "You collect your messages."

Kristin crossed to the telephone and contacted the desk.

"Ms. Allen? This is Marcie at the front desk. Mr. Kendrick called while you were out. He asked me to give you the message that he won't be returning to the Circle K tonight as planned, so he regrets that he will be unable to keep his appointment with you."

"Oh. . .okay," Kristin said, as she heard in reality the message that had been a hidden worry in her heart all afternoon. "Thank you, Marcie!" she said in a bright, upbeat tone that she hoped didn't convey her disappointment. She didn't want it passed on if a callous, caddish Dacian Kendrick should inquire of the girl at the desk what Ms. Allen's reaction to the message had been.

"Anything important?" Mandy asked.

She popped the top from the aluminum can, then was forced to take a quick sip before it could bubble over and spill to the carpet. She divided it between two glasses on a tray on Kristin's dresser.

"Or is it none of my business?" Mandy suggested in a rueful tone when Kristin didn't immediately reply.

"The girl at the front desk told me that Dacian had tried to contact me while we were out, so he left a message with her that he's not returning to the ranch, so he can't keep our, and I am quoting now, 'appointment.'"

"Kind of a stilted word for a date, isn't it?" Mandy mused. "Oh well," she said. "You don't know that 'appointment' was Dacian's choice. That may have simply been the word the girl at the desk selected to get the jist of the message."

"I suppose. But—"

And suddenly, Kristin was helpless to contain the worries and insecurities that had plagued her all afternoon, and she blurted to Mandy that maybe it was just a perverse cat-and-mouse game on Dacian Kendrick's part.

"Whatever are you talking about?" Mandy asked.

"He could be toying with me," Kristin said and felt her lower lip tremble. "He could be building me up only to purposely let me down, laughing all the while."

"Don't say such things, Kristin. Don't even think them. They're not true."

"How do you know they aren't?"

"How do you know that they are?"

"Well, Janice did say—"

"I'd call Janice a wicked, lying, envious, troublemaking witch," Mandy said, "except that she's your sister, so I won't."

"In a backhanded way, Mandy, I think that you just did."

"Are you angry with me?"

"I probably should be, but I'm not. I've never been one to argue with the truth," Kristin said and gave a weary sigh.

"So what are you going to do about tonight?" Mandy asked.

"Stay home, do my nails, and read some more on a novel I began on the way here."

"I think that's a mistake. You should go. I want you to go. You can chum around with Billy Joe and me."

"But I don't want to go, not all by myself."

"Billy Joe's got friends. Cute ones, too. Maybe they're not Dacian Kendrick, but they're nice guys."

"I'd sooner stay home than try to be good company, Mandy,

when I feel like I'd be anything but pleasant and charming to be around."

"You've got to go," Mandy insisted.

Kristin noticed a grimness about Mandy and a determined set to her lips.

"But why?"

"Just in case it *is* some kind of ugly trick, Kris, then you'll be out having fun and Dacian Kendrick won't get so much as a moment of satisfaction in thinking of you alone and lonely, eating your heart out over him, while he tears your heart out to get even with your sister."

"You believe me, don't you?" Kristin said. "You think it's possible, too, don't you?"

Mandy nodded. "Possible, yes. Likely, no. Billy's told me Dace is a committed Christian, but we believers can all have our moments of falling flat on our faces, being unacceptably petty, because we are human, after all. . . ."

"Maybe I will go with you," Kristin said. "And I'll just put Dacian Kendrick from my mind and concentrate on having a great time."

"Good girl," Mandy said and gave Kristin an encouraging pat on the shoulder. "Don't go off half-cocked, Kris. Don't think about it any more tonight, okay? Wait until tomorrow. Everything may look different then."

# six

Kristin had felt a sense of trepidation when she tagged along with Mandy and a welcoming Billy Joe. But as soon as they neared the site where workhorses were hitched to racks billowing with fluffy straw, she was glad she'd gone along. She wasn't the only person who wasn't part of a couple.

A worker from the ranch's kitchen staff was carefully tending a bonfire. In coolers laid out on picnic tables were uncooked hotdogs, hamburger patties, and other snacks that would be awaiting the guests when they arrived back at the headquarters of the Circle K Ranch.

"All aboard!" the lead wagonmaster said and snapped the reins over the broad backs of a matched team of Belgian draft horses.

Harnesses clinking, massive heads bobbing, they stepped out, their gigantic hooves raising soft swirls of dust into the hazy evening sky flickering with fireflies lifting from the grassy knolls as stars gleamed in the night.

"Nice, isn't it?" Mandy whispered and grinned at Kristin from where Mandy was in the loose circle of Billy Joe's arms.

"It is pleasant," Kristin said, feeling a pang of disappointment that Dace wasn't beside her, snuggled on the soft bed of straw, with him leaning close to whisper private jokes and observations in her ear.

When they passed a small grove, Kristin saw a jackrabbit dart for cover. And as they moved into the vast expanse of open range land, a coyote howled and yipped at the moon. The harrowing, haunting sound that lingered in the cool night air made her shiver and feel oddly lonesome although she was surrounded by people.

"I think we could use a song," someone said.

"Well, we're in luck," one of the ranch hands called out. "Billy Joe Blaylock's got his git-fiddle here somewhere."

Billy, who'd been centering his attention on Mandy, was brought into the spotlight. He tried to protest, but the wagonload of guests and ranch employees wouldn't take no for an answer, and with Mandy's adoring eyes encouraging him, he gave in and agreed to provide the entertainment.

He retrieved his guitar from its sturdy but battered carrying case, quickly tuned it, and then as his calloused fingertips caressed the wires, sliding along the ornate fretwork of the instrument's neck, people began to join in and sing old favorite familiar songs.

The wagons that had drawn ahead of the one where Kristin, Mandy, and Billy Joe were riding, slowed their pace to narrow the gap, and soon it sounded like almost everyone from the Circle K Ranch was serenading the harvest moon that rose high and huge overhead.

If the coyotes mourned in the night, the guests of Dace Kendrick's dude ranch, including Kristin, were too boisterously happy to even notice.

"I need something to drink," Mandy said when they returned to the ranch and hopped down from the wagons, brushing straw from their clothes and hair.

"Me, too."

"I haven't done that much singing since, since--"

"Kindergarten?" Kristin supplied, feeling another stab when she remembered holding hands and swinging along with Dace.

"Probably," Mandy acknowledged. "But hasn't it been fun?"

"Perfect," Kristin said.

Mandy frowned. "Well, not quite perfect, Kris, because your guy wasn't able to be here."

"I don't want to think about that tonight. Remember?" Kristin said.

"Sorry," Mandy murmured. "I was just having so much fun that I—I—"

"Don't apologize, Mandy. I know that you want me to have what you do. And from my point of view. . .it looks like you have a man who loves you."

"Oh, do you think so, Kris? I've thought that, too, but then I've remembered what your sister told you about the insincere, smooth-talking men at dude ranches, then I hardly dare hope."

"My dear, there is nothing insincere about the way Billy Joe looks at you. Mandy, his eyes regard you as if he thinks that the sun rises and sets on you, and the oceans calculate their tides by your desires."

Mandy gave a delighted giggle.

"He does act pretty sweet on me, doesn't he? And I'm *crazy* about him. I know that my family would be, too."

"Billy's easy to like. So nice. So thoughtful. Intelligent."

"Just about everything a girl could ever want," Mandy murmured, her tone wistful.

The two fell into momentary silence as they stood off by themselves and Billy was occupied helping the other ranch employees put the Belgians in their pasture.

"Kris. . .can I ask you something?"

"Sure."

"Do. . .do you think that what I feel for Billy Joe could be love? Or do you think that it'll go away? Die like a cruise ship romance does as soon as a person steps on dry land?"

"I don't know, Mandy. I'm not exactly experienced when it comes to matters of the heart."

"I feel different this time. Real different." She paused and when she spoke again, there was a catch in her voice. "I've never had a life other than the one with my family and friends in Kirkwood, where I feel like I'm marking time hunched over a keyboard tapping data into the company's terminals. I. . .I . . .well, since meeting Billy Joe, and getting to like him as I do, I realize that I don't want to go back to that life. I've always believed that God had plans for me since He laid the very foundations of the universe. That there was a special man for me, desired for me by my Lord and Savior, and that given time God would lead me down a path so I'd meet that man, and perhaps I wouldn't recognize him instantly, but that the Lord would open my eyes so I'd see him as the perfect mate for me, and he would see in me the woman cherished and desired above all others. I want to stay right here. But I can't. This week will be up in a wink, then there's next week, and after that I have to pack my bags, climb in the van, head for the airport, and. . . . Kris, I'm afraid maybe this isn't meant to be, and I want this to be God's plan for me!"

Mandy, who Kristin realized, was too choked up to speak further, fell silent. Kristin put her arm around the shorter girl's shoulder and gave her a comforting hug.

"Don't think about the tomorrows, hun," she advised. "Just live for the moment. Make it through the here and now and the future will take care of itself. If it's meant to be, it'll happen. If not, perhaps you await a fellow who's even more perfect."

"You know, that sounds like something wise that my mother would say," Mandy said, dabbing at her eyes. "You've just made me feel better. Thanks."

Kristin smiled acceptance of the sentiment, then turned away as Billy Joe rejoined them. She wished that a few small words from someone could make *her* feel as relieved and happy as Mandy did now.

She realized that there were three tiny words that could make her world explode in bright, radiant happiness, like a rocket bursting on the Fourth of July.

If only Dacian Kendrick would hold her close, kiss her tenderly, and whisper the sentiment meant for only her to hear:

*I love you. . . .*

But why should that ever happen? she realized as she walked back to her quarters and prepared to go to bed. For he actually hadn't given her any indication that she was really any more special to him than any other female on his ranch between eight and eighty who was worthy of a bit of flattery to ensure satisfied customers.

To her surprise, Kristin didn't lay awake stewing about it.

After all of the exercise, good food, and fresh air, she toppled into bed and slept as if she'd died.

When Kristin awoke the next morning, she was considering getting up early so that Mandy wouldn't have to wait for her, when the telephone beside her bed purred.

She got it before the second ring.

It wasn't Mandy, as she had expected, nor was it Dace as she'd fleetingly, wildly hoped. It was the girl at the front desk, this time a different one, Sonya.

"Just checking to see if you're awake, Ms. Allen," the girl said in a pleasant tone. "There was a package left for you at the front desk early this morning. I didn't want to send someone to deliver it and disturb you."

"Oh, that was thoughtful," Kristin said, as she wondered what could have been dropped off at the front desk for safe-keeping.

"You're up and about so I can send someone over with it, then?" Sonya inquired.

"Yes. I'll be waiting."

"Very well. Someone will be there in a jiffy."

Kristin scarcely had time to slip into her robe, brush through her hair with quick motions, and rub the sleep from her eyes before there was a knock at her door.

The young ranch employee checked the number on Kristin's door, then consulted the note on the ornately wrapped package.

"This is for you!" The cute teenage boy announced.

"Thanks," Kristin said.

"Have a nice day, Ma'am," the young cowboy said and tipped his hat.

The realization that the package could only be from Dace immediately made Kristin's day much nicer.

There was another knock at Kristin's door as she seated herself in an occasional chair, the heavy but compact box on her lap. She opened the sealed envelope with her name scrawled on it in what she felt certain was Dace Kendrick's handwriting. It seemed to perfectly represent him: large, well-formed, strong, but distinctively his own. Then there came a knock at the door.

"Just a moment," Kristin called and set the package aside as she rushed to answer. She opened the door to Mandy.

Feeling suddenly on top of the world she gave her friend an impulsive hug and pulled her into the room.

"I swear, Mandy, if you were a little robin, you'd definitely have all the worms. You're such an early bird!"

"Well, you're in a good mood this morning," Mandy said. "Something happen?"

"I think so."

"You think so? You don't know?"

"I got a package," Kristin breathlessly explained. "I think it's from Dace. And I'll know in a moment."

"Wow, the roses have really opened up overnight, haven't they?" She gave a giggle. "I feel almost like I'm in Pasadena on January first instead of in South Dakota the tail end of July."

Kristin hardly heard her as she carefully opened the envelope.

> *Dear Kristin,*
> *I was disappointed not to be able to keep our*
> *date last night. Something came up. I had to*
> *consult with my lawyer in a meeting that went on*
> *endlessly. My body and mind were with him, but*
> *my heart was with you.*
>
> > *Dace*

"Oh, Kristin, see?!" Mandy gave a gleeful squeal. "I told you so. We shouldn't have doubted him for a moment. You know, a place like this spread doesn't run by itself. Someone has to be in charge and make a lot of decisions. And if there are problems, that same someone has to handle them whether it's convenient or not."

"That's true," Kristin admitted, and recalled what Dace had said about how demanding his position had been. What it had cost him over the years, the things he'd been denied that others took for granted.

"What's in the box?" Mandy said.

"We'll see," Kristin said.

She slid a fingernail under the transparent tape, freed the glittery foil paper, and folded it back to reveal the bottom of what was obviously a box chocolates.

"Roses. Chocolates. What comes next?"

"Who knows?" Kristin said, laughing.

She upended the box of candy on her lap, righted it, saw the label and gasped, dismayed.

Mandy misunderstood. "Wow, do you have any idea how much those chocolates *cost?*" She asked in an awed tone.

Kristin felt suddenly sick to her stomach at seeing the label, a little known but famous brand among chocolate afficionados.

"Yes, when I used to live in New York City, I knew their price right on down to the ounce."

"You had a real sweet tooth, huh?"

"No," Kristin said in a careful tone. "I had a big sister who couldn't resist them and had me pick them up regularly on my way home from the modeling agency offices."

Mandy made a strangled sound of compassionate shock. "Oh, Kristin. . . ."

"These chocolates just happen to be Janice's all-time favorites."

"Really, Kris, they're an excellent, expensive brand. The kind that you'd give to someone you want to impress. The fact that your sister was addicted to them and Dace decided to give that brand to you doesn't mean a thing."

"Doesn't it?" Kristin murmured.

"Does it?" Mandy countered.

"I don't know," Kristin said. "And I wish I did. It's driving me crazy, not knowing where I stand with Dacian. Wondering one moment if he sees in me the woman of his dreams. And worrying the next instant that he views me as the perfect instrument for his revenge. . . ."

By that evening Kristin had gone from wondering about Dacian's intentions regarding her to feeling that she was the most important woman not only in South Dakota, but in the entire world as far as he was concerned.

For once she happened to be in her room when a call came for her, and she took it, suspecting that it might be Mandy, who was too comfortable to get up and walk to the room next door. Or perhaps, she worried, it was a call from Janice.

When Kristin found Dace on the line her heart skipped a beat and then her pulse accelerated. She was unable to keep the joy from her voice, and from the way his tone warmed and grew intimate as a caress, Kristin realized he'd noticed and was pleased by her reaction.

When he began to tell her how much he had missed her and how he'd thought of her for what seemed every waking moment when he wasn't occupied with intricate business concerns, Kristin felt as if she'd never been happier in her life.

"You don't have forever here at the Circle K," Dace pointed out, momentarily breaking her heart as he presented the reality she'd tried to forget. "So we're going to make the most of what time you have here, starting tonight. What would you like to do?"

"Well, I've tentatively promised that I'd go out with Mandy, and her boyfriend. . .Billy Joe. Billy Joe Blaylock."

"We could all go out together," Dace suggested. "Do you think they'd be interested? Billy's a lot of fun."

"So is Mandy."

"You set it up then," Dace ordered, "and that's what we'll do. Tell them it's my treat."

"Okay. Do you have anything specific in mind?" Kristin asked. "So they'll know what to plan?"

He paused a moment. "The other night was one of the most memorable of my life. Care for an encore?"

"I'd love it."

And Mandy, when she sampled nightlife in Rapid City, South Dakota, did, too.

"I wish this vacation would never end," she sighed when she and Kristin went to the powder room to check their makeup.

"I know," Kristin said and felt a twinge of sadness. "But life goes on. There's no stopping it."

"I'd like to try," Mandy said. "If I could get a job out here, with the least little encouragement from Billy, I'd move to South Dakota bag and baggage to remain near him.

Kristin couldn't help smiling.

Mandy caught Kristin's expression in the mirror and looked stern. "I'm serious, Kris. I'm not clowning around. In my heart," she said and touched the bodice of her pretty, slimming dress, "I feel as if Billy Joe could be the one. The man for me."

"I know," Kristin said. "And some of the looks I've intercepted tonight have seemed to express that Billy Joe feels the same way about you."

"But he's so shy and so steadfast and so sober and so careful, he won't give me encouragement to find a way to stay out here, even if he wants to. Not until he can promise me all the security that a guy like Billy would feel that he should offer a woman before he'd. . . ." Her words trailed off to a sigh.

"I know," Kristin said. "I can tell that he's that kind."

"And bold as I can be sometimes," Mandy lamented, "I just don't have it in me to throw myself at him. I'd die if he told me to go back to Kirkwood. That I was just another summer romance."

"I don't think he would. Give him time."

"That's one thing that I don't have. And that I can't afford to buy. I have no more vacation time with the company. And I saved all year long to pay the rates this place charges."

"Don't fret over it, Mandy. Perhaps something will come up. You can't let the fact that you may have to leave destroy enjoyment of what time you do have left."

"That's true," Mandy agreed in a morose tone.

"I'm not exactly feeling so perky myself in that area," Kristin admitted. "Our two weeks are up on the same day."

"I know. We can leave together. Misery loves company, they

say. But somehow, I have a feeling that Dace is going to be asking you to stay. Kris—the man can't take his eyes off you. He stares at you like he's in a trance. Like someone's dinged him on the head, only instead of seeing stars, he's seeing hearts, flowers, butterflies, and hearing bells. Maybe even wedding bells!"

Kristin's heart lurched.

That was exactly what she'd thought, earlier, but then she'd given herself a mental talking to and told herself that it was an incorrect assessment, one produced by her hopeful mind and romantic heart.

"We've still got over a week left in South Dakota," Kristin pointed out. "We've got lots of time to have fun. And maybe even enough days, hours, and special moments for a miracle to happen for each of us."

"Do you think so?"

"I hope so," Kristin said. "In fact, maybe I even know so."

"What are you getting at?"

"Ummm. Something for me to know. . .and you to find out," she teased.

And Kristin made a mental note that at the first opportunity possible, when she and Dace were alone, and he was in the right kind of mood, she was going to mention Mandy's plight, and hope that a kind, generous, caring man like Dacian Kendrick might find a way to employ a competent girl like Mandy, so that she could remain at the Circle K, a paid employee instead of a pampered guest. But either way, near the man she loved.

For a swift, secret moment, Kristin lamented that she didn't have someone to plead the same consideration on her behalf.

When her two weeks were up, home she would have to go.

For she couldn't ever humiliate herself by hinting for a job so that she could stay. For although her bank account could stand it, her pride could never afford for her to pay the Circle K's daily rate to be near the man she felt drawn to, dare she call it love, in a way she'd never felt before.

## *seven*

The next few days were like heaven on earth for both Kristin and Mandy.

Mandy spent her daytime hours with Kristin, when Kristin wasn't with Dacian, and wiled away each evening with an attentive Billy Joe as they took part in the square dances and other special social events that the Circle K offered to entertain guests.

Both girls maintained long days, arising early for a delicious breakfast and morning ride. They even tried their hand at tennis, neither of them very good, before they adjourned to the mini-golf course. Then they cooled off with a swim as the day heated up with a vengeance.

Their second week was quickly starting to draw toward a close when one morning Mandy didn't appear on Kristin's doorstep, all ready to go.

Kristin waited awhile, then, afraid that something was wrong she stepped outside and knocked on Mandy's door.

"Just a minute," she Mandy called out in a weak, warbling, tear-stained tone.

A moment later she opened the door and wordlessly gestured for Kristin to step into her quarters. She hadn't begun to get ready for the day.

"You've been crying!" Kristin gasped. She'd scarcely ever seen the girl with anything but a lovely smile on her sweet face.

Mandy managed an embarrassed, wet-eyed grin that quickly faltered toward a sob. "It seems as if that's become a morning greeting. I remember remarking that to you one day."

Mandy, an ordinarily cheerful, optimistic girl, tried for

levity, but failed, as she turned away and helplessly brushed tears from her cheeks, swallowing at sobs that caused her shoulders to heave.

Kristin impulsively put her arms around her unhappy friend. "Mandy, please don't cry. It breaks my heart to see you like this."

Mandy's face crumpled. "Well it b. . .b. . .breaks my heart every time I think about going home to Missouri. And Billy's not himself, either. He's as miserable as I am. But we're at a point where neither of us knows what to do. Maybe there is nothing to do. I talked to Mom and she says that it's my life and my decision to make, because she wants only the best for me and to know that I'm happy. I wish I knew what to do."

"Hope for a miracle. And enjoy the moments together. Anyway, if you have to go back to Missouri, Mandy, you can still come out for a holiday vacation, or surely next summer. It won't mean being apart forever."

"Yeah," Mandy said, brightening a little bit.

"Let's go get some breakfast," Kristin said. "You'll feel better after we have something to eat. Afterwards we'll go for a ride."

"I'm getting good enough that I never get Molly any more," Mandy said. "And I miss her. I wonder if she misses me?"

"Let her out of the corral with a novice rider and it'll become clear she misses her real home the most. She must have a wonderful home."

"And master or mistress."

Mandy seemed to perk up as they set about their day's activities.

All week long Kristin had been letting the matter coast along, waiting for Dace to be in exactly the right frame of mind when she made her suggestion. But she knew that she could no longer postpone taking action with Dacian because time was running out.

Undefined concerns had kept Kristin silent all week. She hadn't wanted to risk their relationship by giving Dacian the impression that she was a meddling woman. Or that she was trying to tell him how to run his business. But as overworked as he seemed to be, she convinced herself that she'd actually be doing him a favor and she couldn't believe it would be an imposition to suggest that he might want to at least consider hiring a girl as computer competent as Mandy.

As intuitive as she'd come to realize Dace was, and the way he seemed to like to keep his help happy—and Billy Joe *was* visibly miserable—Kristin was a bit surprised that Dace hadn't seen the straits Billy was in and considered a solution himself.

Of course Kristin realized that Dace was a bit preoccupied. He was busy with last minute details for the arrival of children for the dreams-come-true two weeks of Operation: Recovery and the rodeo. But even so, she'd recognized that there was something about him that caused a worried tenseness to underly his features even when he seemed to be relaxed and was apparently having fun.

She could tell that he was deeply troubled about something. What, she didn't know. And she dared not ask, out of apprehension that it might actually regard her and her worst middle-of-the-night fear that he would uncover the family secret that lay between them.

There were moments when from things Dace said she had felt certain he knew and he was toying with her, to see if she'd be honest enough to admit the situation herself.

Other times, Kristin was so sure that he had no idea Janice was her sister that her heart soared until it as abruptly plummeted when she realized that the fact could not remain hidden forever.

Whatever it was that was bothering Dace, he tried not to let it disturb their times together, and in her heart, Kristin wished that he would confide in her, lean on her a little bit. She wanted him to trust her enough to let his burdens become hers to share . . .even if she found herself unable to believe that he could reciprocate enough for her to be able to count on him to willingly and forgivingly shoulder her problem—Janice—as his own to resolve.

That afternoon when Mandy and Kristin were heading back to their rooms from the swimming pool, Dace exited his office and sought out Kristin.

"I know we have plans for tonight, Kris," he said, after greeting Mandy, too. "But I have to work late in my office. Come there when you get freshened up, and you can wait while I attend to whatever items on my desk can't be ignored a moment longer."

"Okay."

"You don't mind?"

"Of course not," Kristin assured. "I'll bring along a book. Or I could help you if you had something you needed done that I could do. Typing. Filing. That kind of thing."

"What I have to do requires my attention. I know our computer system. You don't, unfortunately."

From the corner of her eye, Kristin saw that Mandy was torn between offering her keyboard services and safeguarding her time with Billy.

Of course Billy Joe won.

"If you can't spare a night away from your work, I'll understand," she said, although the offer was almost unconvincingly delivered as time between them shortened, bringing a quick sting of disappointed tears to her eyes.

"I wouldn't dream of it. Time's passing too fast as it is."

Kristin nodded, relieved, but was suddenly unable to speak as she was struck by how little time remained.

"See you later," Dace said and rushed back to his work.

It was late afternoon and Mandy was primping for her night with Billy Joe when Kristin walked along the pathways to the building that housed the lobby, front desk, Dacian's office, and the gift shop and other businesses.

Dace was on the phone when Kristin gave a light rap on the open door.

Wordlessly he gestured for her to enter.

She sat down, opened her book, but actually watched him as

he frowned, listened to his caller for a long time, made undecipherable responses, and ended up agreeing to table the matter for awhile and take no action at present.

"Made yourself comfortable, Kristin?" he asked as he hung up. "Can I get you anything? Coffee? Tea? Soda? Perrier?"

"Nothing, thanks. Don't go to any trouble on my account. Just attend to your business. I can wait here. Or. . .if I disturb you I could go wait in the lobby."

"Don't be silly. Of course you don't disturb me. Well, actually you do," he said, giving a light laugh. "As pretty as you look it's hard to concentrate on the work I have to do. But I wouldn't have asked you here if I hadn't wanted you with me. I'll try to hurry."

"If there's anything I can do to help—"

"I wish there were, but there's not. Now, if you'll excuse me I'll rush through these contracts and then we can. . . ."

His words trailed off as Kristin turned back to the novel she had brought along, and she opened it to where she'd placed the bookmark, but the words swam before her eyes. She was lost in another world and swirling in conflicting emotions as she considered the near future and knew that the time was coming when she would have to leave no matter how badly her heart ached to stay.

And from remarks Dace had made, hints, could it be true that he might actually want her to remain? Even if he did, how?

Suddenly Kristin was lost in thoughts to the point where she stared unseeingly at the page. She was unaware of the passage of time until Dace rolled his chair away from his desk, shut the center drawer, put his pen in its holder, and snugged his chair up against the shiny mahogany desk as he reached for his Stetson on a hat rack.

"Ready to go?" Dace asked, snapping her from her musings.

"Yes. Right away," she said and arose, slipping the book into her purse as she joined him.

He led the way to the hall, closed his office door behind

them, but did not lock it.

Kristin, who was so security conscious, was startled.

"Don't you lock your office?" She asked. "I should think—"

"Sometimes the people at the desk have a need for something in the office. I have a reliable staff. I trust them."

"Yes, I suppose so."

Dace gave her an amused glance that seemed to become a scrutinizing stare as he considered her reaction.

"I have no secrets," he murmured. "My life is an open book."

And although the words were kindly spoken, Kristin felt herself flinch as if the remark had been a heartless reminder to her that honest as she wanted to be with him, she was a prisoner of deception, with a necessary lie between them in order that another woman's treatment wouldn't tear their relationship apart, leaving her guilty by association.

Kristin was silent as he led the way to his car. He unbuttoned another button on his western shirt, eased his Stetson back on his head, glanced at her, and gave a helpless yawn.

"You're tired," she said.

"A little bit."

"You've been working so hard. You need someone to help you."

He gave an amused laugh. "Needing help and finding the right employee are not always one and the same, my dear."

It was her chance, Kristin realized, the moment that she'd been waiting for, and praying for, turning to God with a trust deeper than she'd attained before Mandy's ideas had edified her own walk in faith, causing it to expand and enrich.

But before she could open her mouth and make a simple suggestion that might be the answer to Dace's problems, he spoke on.

"What do you want to do tonight?" he asked, changing the subject.

"I'm easy to please. Whatever you'd like to do is fine with me."

"A quiet night appeals to me," he admitted, pausing. "I told you once that I'd take you to my place, my haven. Not very many people have been allowed there. It's where I go to relax. Want to see it? We could fix ourselves something to eat there. Maybe grill out."

She took his hand and squeezed it. "I'd love to see your house. A quiet evening sounds wonderful. You keep us so busy at the Circle K. This'll give me a chance to catch my breath. I feel like I've been caught in a whirlwind for the past week and a half."

"Then it's settled. I have steaks in the freezer, a gas grill, everything for a super meal."

"That'll be enjoyable. And I am hungry."

"You can do the salad while I prepare the steaks. After we finish our meal we'll have the whole evening together."

"Maybe we could go for a moonlight ride," Kristin said.

"Ordinarily, yes, but at the moment I don't have a horse on the place," Dace admitted. "Although if you really want to, I could call over to the Circle K and have them load a pair into the horse van and they could be here within minutes."

"There's no sense going to all that bother. There's always tomorrow. I'll be riding with Mandy in the morning."

"Then tonight is ours."

At the remark, said in a tone so soft and sensual, Kristin's heart thumped as she wondered if Dace was setting the scene for a seduction. While she wanted him to kiss her again, as he did each night, holding her hand in a possessively thrilling way, she wasn't sure exactly what he had in mind. With Mandy's talk of Dace being a Christian, Kristin had faith he wouldn't try to press beyond certain boundaries.

From things he'd said, and from remarks others had made, and surely at his age, he wasn't as totally inexperienced as she was, and she feared that he might be prepared to ask of her more than she was comfortable with. Or would he?

She felt a little shiver of fearful anticipation, but when Dace gave her arm a tender pat, seeming unspeakably happy just to have her beside him in his flashy car, she drew from the companionable touch the knowledge that he wanted to be with her to share. . .not selfishly take from her. . .and she felt a surge of renewed trust for him. He wasn't that kind. But Janice certainly was! Could he be a hypocritical Christian? A chameleon? Showing different colors depending on whom he was with at the moment?

However their evening progressed, no matter what his desires became, she knew that if she asked him to stop. . .he would.

They passed along the rural roads that she'd been on before in the ranch's van and in Dacian's Corvette. Instead of proceeding toward Interstate 90 they turned onto a side road. It wound around a curve, then another, and as they rounded a bend and crested the hill, Dacian's private residence came into view.

It was a big house, but not so huge that it would be difficult for a person to maintain it without help, Kristin's Roving Maid personality realized. It looked to be a house that a person would maintain with a sense of proud fulfillment.

The grounds were beautifully kept with bright flowers, pleasant shrubs, and majestic shade trees. The landscaping accentuated the graceful line of the gently rolling lawn that disappeared into pasture land beyond pristine white board fencing marking the perimeter of the acreage.

A fenced-in private swimming pool graced the rear of the house. A bright red barn was obviously a stable for a riding horse or two, although they did seem somehow empty, with no horses standing in the shade, no welcoming nicker when they arrived.

"Oh, Dacian. . .it's like heaven on earth. You must love it here."

"I do," he admitted. "I had it specially designed and built to suit my specifications. It's handy. It's close enough to the Circle K to be convenient, but far enough away to be serene. And my staff has orders not to disturb me here except in an emergency. Come," he said, and helped her out. "Let me show you around, then I'll start the steaks and you can start making the salad."

The matter-of-fact, sharing way he laid out the plans, so that they each contributed as equals, made Kristin's heart wrench. She realized now what so many other young women her age had as they built a life together with a man they loved, and shared the joys, the sorrows, the work, the leisure. And children. . . .

Dace's explanations drew her thoughts away from her private musings as he showed her around his spread, and then took her to the house, which Kristin was relieved to learn that he *did* keep locked.

Fifteen minutes later Dace took two T-bone steaks from the freezer and turned on the gas grill while Kristin fixed a tossed salad in his beautiful, convenient, but quaint country kitchen, a room that was so charming and warm that she had no doubt she was welcome to work there. She looked around and realized that it was a kitchen just like she'd have had designed for herself if she'd been granted every whim, with her smallest wish the contractor's command.

They were enjoying their meal when Dace's telephone rang, disturbing the atmosphere.

"I hope it's not an emergency from the ranch," Kristin murmured.

"Probably not. They haven't called in ages. And this is an unlisted number. So it won't be someone trying to sell me windows, vinyl siding, or a newspaper subscription that I'm not interested in purchasing." He made no move to answer, then explained. "I'll let the machine take it. It's probably my mother who's visiting her sister in California. Or maybe one of my sisters-in-law wanting to know why I haven't been showing up at one of my brother's ranches for a home-cooked meal and an evening spent wrestling nephews or dandling nieces on my knee."

Hearing the words, and knowing what a wonderful family life he had, then comparing it with the wasteland that was her kinship, Kris felt suddenly bleak.

Dace cocked his head, listening, when on the fourth ring his recorded message invited the caller to leave a name, number, date and time of call, and a brief message, then finished with the promise that Dace would return the call.

"Dace? This is Matt Briner, I'm making good progress with the investigation. I've incurred some travel expenses. One trip took me all the way to Illinois. But now I'm onto—"

Dace shot from his chair so fast that he almost upended the small table where they were dining into Kristin's lap.

Roughly he hit the button to stop the machine. He snatched the receiver from the cradle and greeted Matt Briner with a hearty voice, although it bore a hint of strain, and Kristin could tell that Dacian Kendrick was extremely upset.

He glanced at Kristin, lowered his voice, then turned his back to her, mumbling. Then he said, "Hang on a minute, Matt."

He turned to Kris and his eyes were funny, a flat hue, as if he were trying to keep them expressionless and unfathomable.

"Kris?" He spoke to her, but didn't wait for her to reply. "It's pleasant on the enclosed porch. This is going to take me awhile. Business. Perhaps you'd like to wait out there?"

It was offered as a suggestion, but she had no trouble discerning it as a direct order.

"Sure," she agreed, even though she felt stung as if she were a banished child, unwanted. "Of course."

Plucking up her plate she felt numb, and her steps were wooden, as she walked from his presence.

She felt a spike of anger surge through her. She considered abandoning her steak and walking out on him. She wasn't a fool. She knew that whatever it was he was talking about, he didn't want her to hear a word of it. And she'd already heard enough. Investigation! Illinois!

She felt pained, miserable, and she glanced at the horizon, not sure how far the Circle K Ranch was from Dacian's private property. They'd had to go out of their way, twisting and turning. As the crow flies, she thought, it couldn't be too far.

She was tempted to strike out walking. She at least was

reasonably dressed for it.

But when she regarded her low, rather unsubstantial shoes, and considered trekking through rattlesnake country in the dark, her angry resolve became fear and stopped her.

Then a lone coyote howl sealed her fate.

She would have to wait on Dacian Kendrick to see her home, like it or not.

He was a man with no secrets? She recalled his remark time and again as he remained on the telephone for an exceedingly lengthy conversation.

"Obviously he lied," she muttered.

Instead of making her feel better, it made her feel even worse when she recalled that she was living her own lie, too. Not on purpose, of course, but because she'd had no choice. Maybe Dacian was caught up in something bigger than he was, too.

Left alone, her steak finally finished, a puddle of dressing in the bottom of her salad bowl, she began to consider what she *had* managed to overhear.

Dace had an investigator working for him.

Obviously it regarded a sensitive matter, the way Dace had sprung from his chair.

And it was serious enough so that the man was free to rack up expenses that weren't small enough to be handled from a petty cash fund. He'd even traveled to *ILLINOIS!*

Kristin's heart stopped beating, then when it picked up it was rapid and arrhythmic. For a long, horrifying instant, she couldn't catch her breath. She felt faint when the full force of the ramifications swept over her.

Why Illinois if not over her?

Suddenly Jan's mocking remarks came back to haunt her.

Had Dacian been so curious about who she really was that he'd hired a private investigator to check her out? To see if she was who she claimed?

Illinois was a big state, long, from the Wisconsin line north of Chicago all the way down to Cairo, where the Mississippi and Ohio Rivers met and merged.

There were all kinds of reasons why Dace could have sent an investigator to Illinois, she tried to convince herself, but she was unable to comfort herself with logic because women's intuition was signaling to her that something, and something awful, was about to happen.

It was only a matter of time.

While she was living for the moment.

A fool enjoying a fool's paradise.

While tragedy waited, poised to strike. . . .

"I'm back," Dace said. "I reheated my steak in the microwave. Want anything for dessert? I think I have some cheesecake in the freezer. I could get it out—"

"No thanks," Kristin said, wondering if he was suddenly conversational because a problem had been solved, or if it was a clever cover-up. Was he trying to prevent her from suspecting that he had a cruel trap in position, just waiting for her to blindly and trustingly blunder into it, so that he could leave her tangled up in a web of humiliating facts, enjoying her hurt and shame as she paid the price for her sister's old sins.

But to her relief Dace seemed in better spirits for the rest of the evening.

"Let's leave the dishes," Dace suggested. "They'll still be here tomorrow when Mrs. Appleton arrives."

"Your housekeeper?"

"Umm-hmmm. She's getting older. She's wanting to retire. I have to jolly her to keep her on the job. And I try to be neat so as not to make too much work for her."

"Which I know she appreciates."

"Spoken like a true Roving Maid," Dace teased.

"Well. . .I do know what it's like. I appreciate clients who treat me like a human being and don't consider that they've just hired an indentured servant, expected to do in one day what would take the employer a week of steady labor."

"If Mrs. Appleton is intent on retiring, I suppose that I could let her go. And you could always apply for her position," Dace said. He seemed to study her. "Mrs. Appleton dresses to suit herself. It's none of my business what she wears, or if she does housework in the altogether, because I'm never around when she's hear. But I think you'd look darling in a maid's uniform—and I might insist."

"Then I won't bother to apply," Kristin warned. "It's Reeboks and jeans for me. No short black dress and frilly white cap and apron," Kristin joked as her heart skittered. "We professional domestic technicians can be an independent lot. We can decide to refuse an account and replace it with a new client immediately. A good cleaning woman deserves to be wooed and won."

"Then perhaps I should practice up a bit," Dace said, "for when Mrs. Appleton gives me my walking papers as a domestic account."

"Maybe you just should!" Kristin warned in a haughty tone, as a smile curved her lips. She was so relieved that he wasn't cranky and cantankerous upon his return from the call as she'd feared he might be.

"In that case. . .I will. But it's been so long since I've seriously wooed. . .I wonder if I remember how. Oh! I think that I do!"

He took Kristin's hand, turned it over, palm up, and placed a tender, feathery kiss in the cup of her hand, closing her fingers around it, as if she could capture and keep it forever.

Then his lips deftly kissed a nibbling trail up to her wrist. The pressure intensified and Kristin wondered if his sensitive lips were pressed against the artery near the bone and he were monitoring her rapidly escalating pulse.

As if he sensed her trepedation, his lightly bussing lips moved up the satiny smooth length of her tanned arm.

"Stop that!" Kristin giggled. "You're embarrassing me."

Dace stopped instantly. "Foiled again. Here I was, thinking that I was managing to woo you, and instead you inform me that I'm only succeeding in embarrassing you. It may be an uphill task to replace dear old Mrs. Appleton when the time comes."

"You could always start doing your own housework."

"Or I suppose that I could get married," he sighed. "It's probably easier to find a wife than it is to locate the ideal cleaning woman."

Then he began to laugh, as if he'd just cracked a joke, and maybe he had, because Kristin knew that there were various people who had relied on agents of different sorts, just as she'd once been aligned to Andre D'Arcy. It was common for them to say that a husband or wife could come and go, but an agent-client relationship could be irreplaceable.

But was he serious, serious about her, when he made mention of marriage? Did he pass the reference off as joking banter so that his heart wouldn't be on the line, out in the open, a target for hurting remarks, if he was cruelly rebuffed? Had he said what he had said to gain a clue to how *she* felt about their newly developing relationship? Had he, too, been lying awake at night, entertaining thoughts that were a perfect match for the dreams that had captivated her to produce thrilling flights of fancy?

*Oh, dear God, could it be the beginning of a miracle, and he'd teased her about wanting her as a maid. . .when he actually was obliquely referring to a desire that she'd agree to one day come to be his wife?*

Goose bumps spread over Kristin's skin. Dace saw, put his arm around her, and drew her close.

"Let me warm you," he said, his voice so loving.

Then his arm slid around her and she felt herself being drawn close, her female softness conforming to his angular male body. He drew her even closer, holding her so close that she could scarcely breathe. Then his lips tenderly covered hers, and his rougher male cheeks sensuously and pleasantly abraided her smooth ones.

When she melted against him, he made a sound of delight that seemed to well from deep within him, and Kristin felt a stab of pleasure that she'd found womanly approval with him.

His fingers splayed at the nape of her neck, smoothing the

thick dark hair, as his questing fingertips caressed her face, her throat, sifted through her hair, then stopped at the small ridge caused by a scar.

He paused a moment, then continued, caressing even that, and she suddenly felt so accepted by him, feeling that he loved her, imperfections and all.

"Oh, Kristin. . .Kristin," he murmured.

She found herself softly whispering his name, too, as she was lost in the pleasure and power found in his arms.

When Dacian was the first to pull away, even when she knew that he did not want to, her heart almost burst because she was so content, knowing that he cared for her to the point where he would not act selfishly, not considering what might happen to her.

"It's getting late, love," he said. "I really should get you back to the Circle K. Ready to go, dear?"

"Whenever you are."

"We could take the long way back to the ranch."

"Sounds nice."

Enroute back, she decided that she couldn't wait for an opening to plead Mandy's cause, she would have to make one. And there was no time like the present.

"Dace. . .the other day, you mentioned that you'd like to expand your computer operations at the ranch," Kristin said. "I know that this really isn't any of my business, yet I. . .I. . . ."

"Go on," Dace urged. "I know anything you'd suggest would be made in good faith, and because you wanted the best for me—"

"It's Mandy," Kristin said. "She's a hard worker, she's a smart girl, she's spent several years working with computers for an insurance firm in the St. Louis area, I know she'd be qualified and everything you could hope for in office help. Could you please consider hiring her?" she finished in a burst of words that left her breathless.

"Hire Mandy? Well, it is an idea, but she already has a job, and—"

"She doesn't want to leave here when her—our—two weeks are up, Dace, and I know that Billy Joe doesn't want her to, either. But she has no choice. She can't remain on as a paying guest. But if you could hire her, she'd be earning money instead of spending it, and. . ."

"I see," he mused. "It really is a good idea. And if she's experienced, it would make it so much easier than trying to train a local girl."

"Plus, Mandy's nice. Pleasant. Thoughtful. Hardworking. And the way she and Billy Joe feel about each other, it's not like you'd get her trained, and she'd up and get married and move off leaving you to retrain someone else. The way things look for Mandy, if you give her a job, Dace, she's here to stay. She's as loyal as they come."

"Sweetheart, I think you just gave me an answer to one of my problems." He sighed. "Too bad the other concerns can't be dispatched with so easily," he added in a bitter tone.

"Then you'll offer her a job?" Kristin said.

"You can take her an application tomorrow; I have plenty of them in the office. Or you can send her in to see me."

"I'd rather not," Kristin said. "I don't want her to know that I asked a favor of you. I think it would make her much happier if she felt that you'd recognized her potential on your own. And you offered a job based on merit alone."

"You're right. And it's really commendable for you to want Mandy to feel that it's her own worth that's been recognized, when so many people would've wanted a friend to be left feeling beholden. Or forever owing a serious favor."

"Mandy will be so happy not to have to go back to Kirkwood."

"And how are you feeling about returning to Camden Corners?"

"Dace, please. Don't even ask. I don't want to talk about it."

"Why I ask is. . .because I think you should stay." He cleared his throat. "You don't have to go back, you know," he said. "You could remain on so that you'd fulfill the contract requirements."

"What?" Kristin asked, puzzled, when the conversation took a sharp turn from matters of the heart to center on business concerns.

"The Happy Trails Feed folks awarded you the Grand Prize. It was two weeks for you *and* a companion. There's only been you. I don't feel right taking the contracted amount from their corporate comptroller without delivering one hundred per cent of our agreed upon services. Which is a total of four weeks. Being a man of high ethics, that would mean that I'd have to refund them a portion of the money tendered. You know how it is in the business world, Kris, you'd sooner provide agreed-upon services than refund monies involved in the deal."

"I see," Kristin said. Her heart leaped at the idea of getting to stay, but sank when she realized how unemotionally Dace was arranging for her to be able to stay.

Couldn't he just ask?

Did he have to go about it as he did? Making her feel that she was but a gambit on a playing board, being moved around by two corporate comptrollers?

Was he just buying time, at the Happy Trail's Feed Company's expense, so that he'd be able to spend more time with her and discern if she really was a woman he could love? Or would prove to be only a pretty facsimile. . .?

"There's only one drawback. The next two weeks the ranch will be full of children, Kristin. They aren't your average youngsters. They're all kids who have been seriously sick. Some of them are disabled. Not one of them will be perfect. And some of them may be so scarred that unthinkingly cruel people would stare. Or worse, turn away in disgust. You might not enjoy it. In fact, you might not even be able to handle it."

"I'll have no problem handling it," Kristin said.

If anything, she was a person who knew what many of them had been through. She empathised with their need for affection and dignity, while a callous world of strangers, sometimes with a glance, or an unthinking remark, tore away their ability to find acceptance in the everyday world.

"You like children?" he asked, as if he hardly dared hope it.

"I love them. At least what contacts I've had with children in the neighborhood. And the youngsters in the homes I maintain while their mothers manage life in the fast lane. The fast lane by rural Illinois standards, that is."

"Great. Then you'll stay? I mean, I know you planned for two weeks away. Can you manage to make it a full month? I know there was some prize money involved to help make up for lost wages."

"I'll manage," Kristin said. "A few telephone calls, Dace, and I can stay as long as I like."

"Then there's no reason in the world for you not to. And if you're worried about your finances and being an idle guest at the Circle K, let me know. Mrs. Moriarty, the head housekeeper for the dude ranch, could always use a willing worker that time of year. Kids aren't as neat as adults, you know. So don't be proud, Kris. Let me know."

"I might just do that. I'm not used to being a lady of leisure," she admitted, and wondered in passing how Janice endured living the stultifying life-style of the idle rich.

"Everything is working out so right," Dace said and on her doorstep swept her into his arms for a quick goodnight kiss. "There's no reason things shouldn't work out."

*Wrong,* Kristin's heart taunted as the kiss lengthened as if they'd just sealed a sacred pact.

There was one reason why she should leave as planned, why she shouldn't risk remaining so that her daydreams could evolve to become the worst nightmares of her life.

*Janice!*

# eight

The next morning when the two girls left the dining hall after breakfast, Dace intercepted them.

Although from outward appearances an onlooker would've thought it was a coincidental meeting, Kristin knew better.

"Mandy," Dace said, after greeting them both, "the other night when we all went out to dinner in Rapid City, I recalled you talking about your job back in Missouri, and that you worked with computers."

"That's right," Mandy said. "For three years now. . .the keyboard, terminal, myriad programs, and I are old friends."

"I've been considering computerizing additional aspects of the operation. Of course the reservations and billing departments are already automated. But there are other areas where we're buried in paper, photocopying, and, well, I was wondering if perhaps you could spare a few minutes to discuss it with me so that I'd really have an idea of our needs before I—"

"Sure," Mandy agreed, before he could speak further. "I'd be glad to help in any way I can and share any insights based on my experiences. When would you like to go over it?"

"Would right now be too much of an imposition?" he asked.

"Well, Kristin and I were about to go riding," Mandy admitted, and she sounded torn between the two choices.

"There'll be horses for us after awhile. I'll be in my room when you're done talking," Kristin said, deciding for her.

Mandy faced Dace Kendrick, cheerfully shrugging.

"Then right now is hunky-dory with me. You can't *believe* how much simpler life can be with all records on computer. Unless, of course, the system crashes. But you institute simple safeguards to try to prevent that from ever happening."

"You sound like you're really computer literate."

"I don't know everything," Mandy quickly clarified in a modest manner. "But you pick up quite a bit of education around the office. The insurance firm makes use of several programs. So I'm familiar with a couple of different systems. I might be able to offer suggestions about the various capabilities—"

"It sounds like Mandy is a walking gold mine of information," Dace said to Kristin. "If this takes longer than we plan, I'll take you both to lunch."

"Okay," Kristin said. "And take your time. Don't concern yourselves over me. I have a book I began on the airplane that I've been meaning to read."

When Kristin returned to her room, Mrs. Moriarty herself was attending to the housekeeping duties in her quarters.

"Hi," Kristin said. "Don't let me disturb you."

"Oh, I can come back later when you're not here," Mrs. Moriarty offered. "I noticed that you tend to vacate your room about this time every day. So that's when we've been attending to things."

"Ordinarily my girlfriend and I usually go riding. But she's meeting with Mr. Kendrick now."

"A nice man," she said. "Salt of the earth."

Kristin listened as one more in a long list of employees sang his praises as an employer.

"I thought you were the girl I'd been seeing with him," Mrs. Moriarty said. "Haven't you been keeping him company?"

"When he has free time."

"Ah, then I don't have to convince you the kind of man he is, do I?" she asked with a laugh. "Do you think you'll stay in touch with him after you leave, Miss Allen? Although I probably shouldn't be asking, since it's really none of my business. But I've noticed that he's been seeing quite a lot of you. And ordinarily, while Mr. Kendrick is very pleasant to the guests, he keeps his distance."

That was news to Kristin, after her own assumptions based on observations of ranch personnel, and what input Janice had told her about how Dacian Kendrick supposedly operated.

"Oh really? Well, I don't know if we'll be in touch or not."

The housekeeper frowned as she dusted ledges.

"I thought perhaps you'd have an idea by now." She consulted a sheet on her clipboard. "You don't have many days left here. We'll miss you."

"I'm afraid you're not so easily rid of me, Mrs. Moriarty."

"Oh?"

"It appears I'll be extending my stay," she explained. "Dace told me about the deal with the Happy Trails Feed Company, and they've paid for four weeks' services here. So I'm going to be remaining on for awhile. Two more weeks. . . ."

"Then you'll be here for Operation: Recovery?"

"Yes. And I'm looking forward to it. It'll probably be one of the most rewarding experiences of my life."

"As I get old and have my trifling aches and pains, sometimes I feel ashamed of myself, complaining as I do, when I'm around those brave children. They're an inspiration to all of us."

"That's what Dace says," Kristin replied. "But apparently he hasn't told you that he did offer me a job if I get bored. And I might without adults to hang around with during the daytime hours."

"Told me what?" Mrs. Moriarty said.

The aging widow who lived at the ranch seemed a bit puzzled, and Kristin sensed that when it came to her housekeeping department, she was a lot like Dace Kendrick, in that nothing escaped her knowledge either.

"That I could be part of the housekeeping staff if I wanted a job to keep me occupied now and then."

"Oh, well that's interesting," Mrs. Moriarty said.

The expression on her face seemed to reveal that she didn't believe Kristin would know one end of the vacuum sweeper from the other.

"It would seem almost like home. You see, I have a free-lance maid service in the town where I live," Kristin added.

"You do?" Mrs. Moriarty asked with fresh interest and the instant empathy found in people who share the same interests or occupation. "You hardly seem the type. You look so pretty, and refined and. . .well, like a model or something."

"Believe me, I now what it is to do hard work," Kristin assured.

"Well if you don't mind, when the children are here, we may put you to work. They're not as tidy as adults, and who'd want them to be? They're here to have fun. Sometimes the housework load escalates. Especially when there are accidents. The children here have their ups and downs. But nothing that Dr. Bill, Dace's younger brother, can't take care of. And Melanie, his sister the nurse. She'll be bringing along Tony, her fiance, this year. But of course you know all that."

"No. . .no I'm afraid I didn't. Dace just. . .hasn't happened to mention it."

Kristin fell silent, realizing that as much as she knew about Dacian, there was as much, or more, that remained hidden from her.

She hardly heard Mrs. Moriarty as she departed and only managed what she hoped didn't seem too perfunctory a reply.

As confident as she'd felt the night before, she no longer felt so sure of herself.

He'd said his life was an open book, but so much had not been shown to her. She hated to pry, what with her own penchant for privacy, but maybe a man like Dacian expected that if his life was like an open book, it was up to someone else to read it rather than have it seem, perhaps egotistically, read aloud.

With that thought Kristin turned back to her novel, but she'd scarcely opened the fluttering pages when there came a brisk tap at her door.

"You in there?" An impatient Mandy called out.

"Coming!" Kristin assured.

"Sorry I was away for so long. I hadn't meant to bend Dace's ear about computers so much. But he was full of questions, and I didn't really have any idea that I was so brimming with technical answers."

"You must've been a big help to him. No doubt he was fascinated."

"We didn't talk the whole time I was gone. He got a call—from some investigator. He put the guy on hold and said that it'd be wonderful if I'd go to the dining hall and bring back coffee, so I did."

"An investigator?" Kristin asked, and her heart clutched in her chest until she almost winced with pain. "I wonder what that was about?

"I haven't the foggiest," Mandy said. "I don't know if he wanted me to get us coffee because he really wanted some—"

"Or to get you out of his office so that he could talk in private," Kristin observed, "to a private investigator, about something he didn't want you to overhear?"

"Right. Although he'd pulled a file while I was gone. And it was on his desk, plain as could be, if I'd wanted to try to read it upside down, I suppose. He didn't act like the paperwork was any big secret."

"Ummmm."

"And in the future I doubt there'll be any secrets kept from me. I just saw Mrs. Moriarty leave," Mandy said. "And guess what, Kris, she's going to be one of my fellow employees of the Circle K Ranch!"

"What?!" Kristin gasped, although Dace had tipped her an unobtrusive wink when he'd led Mandy toward his private offices, so she'd known what was in the offing. "What are you talking about?"

"A job, Kristin. Dace just offered me a job and I accepted. With pleasure!"

"Wait until you tell Billy Joe!"

"I can't wait. Will he be surprised!"

"And happy." Kristin frowned. "Mandy! Are you teasing me? Oh, please don't! This is too good to be true."

"No, I'm not teasing. And you mean you actually had nothing to do with it? That Dacian offered me a job because he really wanted to hire me?"

"It would appear so. Anyway, would I do something like that?"

"Yes you would!" Mandy retorted with a frank assessment. "But I'm glad you didn't have to. Wow, to be asked to work at the Circle K. Dace showed me around, and I'll tell you, I'll be in heaven. I'll have my own little office, not a scrunchy cubicle shared with a zillion other data processors. Dace even said that I might become his office manager, because he has a hunch he'll need one."

"Mandy, I'm so happy for you. I told you to pray for a miracle."

"I did. And I've been hoping and praying for a miracle for you, too. Kris, I don't want you to leave the day after tomorrow."

"Didn't I tell you? No, I guess not, because it slipped my mind. We haven't really had a chance to talk today, but it turns out that I will be staying on for a little while."

Quickly she explained about the Happy Trails Horse Feed deal and the fact that she was welcome to become an employee within the housekeeping department if she wanted to.

"You know, your boyfriend is a really nice guy," Mandy said. "I knew that before, yes, but until my job interview, I didn't know just how nice. He thinks the world of you, Kris. I hope you never do anything to change how he feels about you now."

"Meaning?"

"Don't act innocent, dear. What do you want me to do? Draw you a picture to help you understand?"

"First and foremost, I want you to lower your voice," Kristin said, nervously sinking to her bed as Mandy sat in the chair.

Mandy complied, her tone a hushed whisper, her eyes widening with alarmed concern.

"You can't go on like this, Kristin. I saw a side to Dacian Kendrick that I hadn't really seen before. He's going to be a joy to work with. I can see why his help all speaks so highly of him. He makes clear that he considers us all his equals, that his door is always open to talk if there's a problem."

"Yes. I realized that," Kristin admitted.

She'd noticed that his door was never fully closed, and that help didn't hesitate approaching him with business that needed his immediate attention, or to check with him regarding a matter, or simply to dart in and retrieve something stored in his office. They obviously felt as at ease with him as any employee would hope to feel with a boss.

"He said that he plays square with his help, and that he expects his help to be honest with him. He told me that he knows the computer programs will take me a little while to learn, and he said that he expects slip ups and mistakes to happen, but not to get so worried at the prospect that I'm stressed out to the point I make even more mistakes because I'm nervous."

"That's reassuring."

"And he told me, Kris, that if I make a mistake, especially a bad one that could really cause problems, he wants me to come to him with it right away. He told me that he knows that everyone can make errors. That mistakes can happen to anyone. 'A mistake that simply happens,' he said, 'is the way life goes. We start fresh. But what I don't tolerate is someone making a serious mistake, and then *making a second, even bigger mistake*, in trying to hide it from me.' Unquote," Mandy said and paused. "He told me that he'll never get angry if I'm a big enough person to confess an error. But that he does not tolerate deceit."

"You won't have a problem in the world, then," Kristin assured. "Because you're not that kind of girl."

Mandy was wringing her hands, as if she'd explained the best parts of the morning, but now faced the most difficult. She stared at her lap, then lifted her eyes to give Kristin a penetrating stare.

"I know I'm not the kind of girl, Kris, and neither are you. And *I* don't have a problem. . .but, my friend, *you* really do. And what makes me feel so angry and so helpless is that it's not even your mistake, it's *hers*. After hearing what Dace said, I realized that you're courting disaster by keeping secret the fact that the woman he can't stand is the only sister of the girl he loves."

Miserable silence stretched, the still seeming almost thunderous in the quiet room.

"What do you think I should do?"

Mandy sighed. "Tell him."

"That's easier said than done."

"I know. I don't envy you the prospect. But Kris, you've got to do it. And do it soon. Before—"

"How?"

"God knows," Mandy said. "But you can't risk letting him find out by accident. You've got to find a way, Kristin, you've just got to. The kind of man he is, with ethics that are black or white, no shades of gray for him, I don't know how he'd handle such a deception. Not even from you. . . ."

"Maybe the simplest solution would be to just pack my bags and go home to Camden Corners as planned. And let Dace worry about dealing with the Happy Trails people. . . ."

"That would be the coward's way out. Don't you get tired of running, Kris? And hiding? Trying to avoid unpleasantness by locking the doors, real or imagined, and insulating yourself from the world, so that you can't risk something out there in the big, wide world hurting you?"

"Old habits die hard," Kristin said.

"Don't I know it," Mandy sympathized

Suddenly, Kristin, without any warning, cupped her face in her hands and began to soundlessly cry.

Mandy arose and awkwardly patted her shoulder.

"I'll leave you alone to think it out. To pray about it," Mandy said in a soft, sympathetic voice. "Dace isn't terribly busy this morning. You could go to his office and have a talk with him. In fact, that would be the ideal place for you to confess, now that I stop to consider it."

Mandy crossed the room and retrieved a box of tissues, handing it to Kristin, who wiped her eyes and managed to face her.

"What do you mean?"

"Well, because, it's a sort of public location." Mandy, with a degree of reluctance, began to explain her simple logic. "If he really blows up, he'll have to keep it toned down a bit. He can hardly yell at you in front of everyone on the Circle K Ranch so they overhear him, can he?"

"Oh, Mandy. . . ," Kristin whimpered. "Knowing his temper, yes. Yes he probably could—and would!"

Mandy thought back to the night they'd arrived.

"I guess he could," she was forced to agree.

Kristin's eyes that had been dabbed dry a moment before quickly refilled with tears.

"Me and my big mouth," she said. "Please, would you just go see him? Now? And get it over with? Trust me: it'll be way worse constantly imagining how awful it'll be, rather than doing it, getting it over with, and facing your reality. People who keep canceling their dental appointments suffer way more anxiety and pain than the ones who make an appointment, keep it, and put the event behind them."

"You're probably right."

"Well, I'm going to go to my room for awhile," Mandy said. "And I'd suggest that you go to Dace Kendrick's office."

"I'll think about it," she promised.

And she did think about it.

But she couldn't make herself act.

As one hour passed, then it became two, and that was all she'd meditated on. She knew that she should walk the distance to his office, ask permission to close the door, and in the quiet hush of his office, tell him the truth and get the terrible burden lifted from her mind and off her heart.

But she just couldn't do it. . . .

She realized that she'd reached a decision, probably a bad one, but what seemed the only choice open to her. She prayed that she could keep her act going for two more weeks, at which time she'd return to Camden Corners and take up where she'd left off with her old life, and hope that Dace Kendrick, like herself, would look back on it with fond memories, and then eventually dismiss it as just a summer romance. . . .

*nine*

Kristin was grateful when Mandy didn't inquire if she'd gone to Dace's office to admit her accidental deceit.

But by the way Mandy frowned, Kristin knew that she hadn't been fooled.

As accustomed to sharing their hopes and dreams and their private fears and problems as they were, she realized that Mandy was perfectly aware that she had not attended to the matter, because if she had taken care of it, she'd have told Mandy what had transpired.

That is, if Dace's reaction hadn't been such that everyone on the Circle K would know from the force of his explosion his response to the news that she was Janice's sister. . . .

Two days later Mandy's weeks as a paying guest ended, as did Kristin's initial stay.

The day after that Operation: Recovery began. A school bus donated by the local district was used to go to the airport to collect the children. The ranch's van was used to shuttle children from shorter distances who arrived by bus or train.

Although the ranch was bustling and the employees were temporarily overworked, their smiles held a hint of happy exhaustion, for the childrens' smiles and displays of excitement became rewards beyond description.

At first Kristin had noticed how disfigured some of the children were from surgeries and treatments, and how others wore turbans that seemed to signify they'd undergone unpleasant bouts of chemotherapy and they needed protection from the sun and stares as their hair grew back in again.

Whatever their situations at home, they'd left a world of poor health behind them, and they did their best to manage the fun activities that average children took for granted.

Dace didn't see much of Kristin the first day, but he did manage to find enough time to introduce her to his brother, Dr. Bill, his sister, Melly, and Tony, whom she was going to marry in a Christmas season wedding.

To Kristin's relief, she liked them as well as she did Kerry, who'd become a friend, and she felt as if she hit it off famously with all the various Kendrick offspring. To her delight, they seemed to have passed approval on her, too, because when Dace was occupied arranging details for the rodeo and was forced into switching livestock contractors at what seemed almost the last moment, his brothers and sisters kept her company.

The more Kristin realized that she liked them, the worse she started to feel; her guilt increased by the day. She wasn't just deceiving Dace, but his family as well.

"You haven't said anything to him yet?" Mandy asked, when she and Kristin took their cups of coffee to a quiet corner of the dining hall during Mandy's break.

"Not yet," Kristin sighed.

"What are you waiting for? Christmas? New Year's? Or the Fourth of July?"

"You know, it's not easy," Kristin said, helpless not to be a bit snappish from stress. "If you were in my shoes you wouldn't be so—"

"You don't have to blow up at me," Mandy said. "I know it's not easy. I'd tell him for you, but it's not my place to do it. And I really don't want to throw a monkey wrench into a brand new boss-employee relationship by sticking my noise into other people's business."

"I'd never ask you to. Or allow it. And although it's another deceit, Mandy, I'm going to let Dace think that you had no idea that Janice is my big sister."

Mandy sighed. "Thanks. That's probably for the best."

The way her gaze lowered, then slid away from Kristin's, it was clear to her that Mandy didn't feel any more at ease with a fib than she did.

"I appreciate it. And I understand why it's got to be that way," Mandy spoke a moment later. "But keeping the secret you are from Dace. . .that's courting disaster and tempting the worst possible scenario to come true."

"I know."

"You've *got* to tell him," Mandy insisted.

"Tomorrow. He's got such worries on his mind already today."

"I know. He's had a lot of calls from that fellow who I gather is an investigator. I think it has something to do with the rodeo. And although I'm not certain, maybe even is why Dace switched contractors for rodeo stock. He seemed to act as if he'd accomplished that in the nick of time."

Or that's what he was letting Mandy think, Kristin realized, because he knew that his new office help was also Kristin's best girlfriend, and he didn't want Mandy to feel a sense of divided loyalties and warn Kristin what he'd found out about her, causing her to flee without warning. . . . So that after carefully laying the trap, it would come up empty, and he'd be denied his moment of revenge. He'd be unable to make her pay for her sister's behavior by humiliating and hurting her the way he'd probably not been able to get at Janice, who could be so thick-skinned at times. Beauty lotions aside, she had the hide of a rhino where matters of the heart were concerned.

"Well, see that you do," Mandy said, jerking Kristin back from her momentary musings about Dace's motives. "I'm a firm believer in tomorrows, new dawns, and starting all over. But time does run out, my friend. And you don't have forever."

"Tomorrow," Kristin promised.

"Good girl."

Kristin took a sip of coffee, and then altered her intent as she sighed, "Maybe tomorrow."

But in the upcoming days, that was what she kept reassuringly telling Mandy, and herself, until soon Mandy ceased badgering her about it and only gave her worried looks interspersed with nettled glances.

Kristin noticed that the more closely Mandy worked with Dace, the harder seemed to be the pull of her divided loyalties, as she couldn't help feeling tugged between two opposing viewpoints.

"I hate what you're doing to him, to yourself, and to me!" Mandy protested. "You're driving me crazy!"

"It hasn't exactly been pleasant for me."

"You're going to have to pay the fiddler sometime, Kris. It may as well be now as later. You know that the day of reckoning is going to come. Perhaps it hasn't dawned on you, but it is in your power to select the moment and see to it that Dace is in the right mood and is sympathetic. That's got to be better than having him stumble onto the information, which I'm warning you, can certainly happen. When it comes to making decisions, that man is meticulous. And he's trying to decide if you're the right woman for him."

"Are you trying to tell me something?" Kristin said and thought about the private investigator and the file folder Mandy had mentioned.

"What I've been trying to tell you for weeks: Come clean! Get it off your conscience and out in the open."

"Tomorrow, Mandy. I promise," Kristin said wearily.

"I wish I could believe you. But I no longer do."

"That's what I'm afraid Dace is going to say if I tell him about Janice, that I'm not like her, and that it doesn't have to be important, that we don't have to let the past, and her, come between a future and us."

"That's an excellent way to put it, Kris."

She wiped a sudden tear that strayed to her cheek. "Have you any idea how many times I've had the conversation in my mind?"

"Then pretend it's a dress rehearsal, instead of the real thing, pretend you're acting a part in the play, and go into his office and put on the performance of your life."

For a harrowing moment Kristin was tempted to do just that, because Dace had been in a super mood that morning after having come in from watching the children being carried around on Molly's back.

Then when she considered what could happen, she lost her nerve.

"Tomorrow."

"Tonight, Kris," Mandy said, as if they were bidding against one another.

Kristin shook her head. "Tomorrow. I won't be seeing him tonight. He's got a meeting in Rapid City."

"That's right. I forgot. Then tomorrow it's got to be."

"And it will. Come morning, Mandy, I promise, I'm going to clear the air so that I can stop living a lie."

She hoped that with the sun's new dawning, she wouldn't find that all resolve would flee again, just as surely as the morning haze was burned away beneath the sun's relentless glare.

But once more, time was running out. Her stay at the Circle K Ranch compliments of the Happy Trails Horse Feed Company would soon come to an end. And she would have to leave. Unless Dacian Kendrick decided to ask her to stay.

She had only known Dace for three weeks. But in some ways it seemed like at least three months, or three years, or the majority of her whole life. And at other moments as if she'd known him forever.

"Forever," Kristin murmured as she watched Mandy deposit her empty cup in a tray, and then lost sight of her as she rounded a corner to disappear into Dace's office.

Forever was what Kristin realized she wanted so very, very much. And she sensed that it was hers for the taking, if only she dared to risk it all and go for it.

"Tomorrow," she promised herself, as she drifted off to sleep, more tired than usual from a long day helping Mrs. Moriarty with the children's quarters. "I'll tell him tomorrow. . . ."

Late that night after spending the evening with Dr. Bill, Kerry, Tony, and Melanie, it seemed as if Kristin had scarcely returned to her quarters, readied for bed, and fallen asleep before there was a pounding on her door.

It wasn't Mandy's knock, she knew. Now that her friend worked at the ranch, she had been assigned a room in a dormitory building. Plus, Mandy didn't keep late hours now that she had to be at her desk early.

The first knock had been harsh.

The raps that followed after it bowed the door beneath a rough, battering, determined pummeling.

"Open up!"

"Just a minute!" Kristin called in a quaking voice. "Who—"

She wasn't about to open her door to an out-of-control madman. She was about to dial the front desk and request help, when she recognized that it had been Dace's fury soaked tone.

"Open up before I kick the door in!" he growled.

Kristin staggered from her bed, drew on her robe, and when she went to the door, not sure she'd get there before Dace somehow tore it off its hinges, she was shivering from the cool night air and her nerves.

Dace flipped on the light, gave her a long look, an infuriated glare, that was so heated she felt an unpleasant warmth flood to her skin. She knew it was a flush of alarm, and shame, of course, but for a moment it had seemed to arrive with the force of Dace's blistering stare.

"What an actress you are," he said, and the mocking words seemed to whistle from him. "Perhaps I should nominate you for an Academy Award. Playing the part of the sweet, lovable, innocent young thing, who's so pleasant and agreeable, when it's clear that you must have a mind like an adding machine, a heart like a cash register, the ethics of a con man, the plans of a swindler, and the bartering skills of a harlot!"

"What are you talking about?" Kristin asked, stalling for time in which to try to shake the sleep from her, as it seemed as if her mental acuities had fled, leaving her without the capacity to provide a convincing, calming defense.

At that moment she felt certain that Dace *had* retained a private investigator to poke into her background, and now he knew the truth after keeping the appointment that took him from her that very night. But a moment later from the hand held behind him he produced an answering machine identical to the one she'd seen at his house.

Without bothering to ask permission, he bullied his way into her room, took over as if she had no right to be there, and plugged the device into a wall socket.

"Listen you vixen," he hissed the order.

Then he savagely punched the button and fumbled to turn up the volume.

Kristin felt her face drain pale as the messages began, and she swirled in an eddying tide of confusion, because none of it made any sense. The messages were just so much gibberish. The evening's calls to his private number meant nothing to her.

"Why are you subjecting me to this?" she demanded to know, her shock and fear giving way to her own fury.

"Be still and listen!"

Then she heard it.

A voice she'd listened to so many times before. Words couched in an accent as phony as the woman who used it!

"Dace, darling, how good to hear your voice, even if it is only on a machine. I've been trying and trying to reach my little sister at the Circle K ranch. But every time they connect me with her room, no one answers. I decided not to bother with leaving a message at the desk, so I looked in my Rolodex, found your unlisted number, and decided to call your home. I thought that perhaps Krissie would be with you there. . .the way we used to be. I trust you can give her my message? As according to Krissie, it's certain that you'll be seeing her because you've been charming her and keeping her very busy indeed, just as you were so wonderful to me last summer when Cissy and I stayed at your ranch. So please tell Krissie that Aunt Dee and Uncle Benchley are in New York City now, and we'll be in touch and to expect our call. Or if she likes, she could telephone us at her earliest con—"

The rest of Janice's message was soon lost in a sickening

flurry of kissypoo good-byes that, by the darkening expression that draped to his story features, apparently infuriated Dace to the degree that it sickened Kristin.

"No wonder you look alike. Two peas in a pod. You sprang from the same bloodlines. *Sisters!*" he spat the word. "You're as deceitful as Janice is. But why should I be surprised? After all, the fruit doesn't fall far from tree, does it? God knows the kind of woman your mother was."

Kristin felt the urge to slap him. "You leave my mother out of this. She's been dead for some ten years."

Kristin fumbled, tried to find words to defend herself and her parentage, to explain, but Dacian was insatiable. There was no stopping him, and she realized no way to excuse her actions.

"What are you? On the prowl for a rich husband? And Janice is siccing you onto the trail in search of her castoff beaus? While she goes on to hunt for bigger game?" He called Kristin a gold digger, and other unflattering names. "You're just like your heartless sister."

"I'm not like Janice!" Kristin cried.

"You're more like her than I'm sure even you can see! Fool me once, shame on you. Fool me twice, shame on me. A year ago Janice and her rich divorcee friend showed up. Your sister threw herself at me. It wasn't until I was stupid enough to impulsively ask her to marry me, that she ended up revealing what she was really like. She was like something unpleasant to behold, that was wrapped up in pretty packaging to fool the consumer. I couldn't believe it when she started offering herself up, for a price, like merchandize for barter. She was interested in marriage, but only on her terms. Trying to flimflam me with phony words of faith that she didn't really possess, and had I been hoodwinked by then, would've found myself unevenly yoked to an unbelieving, wanton woman. . . ."

"I'm sorry," Kristin whispered.

And she was. She knew what Janice at her best was like. She could only imagine her at her worst.

"I'm not so hard up for a woman to love that I had to even consider settling for a plastic personality, and a woman with dollar signs in her eyes, and probably all of the mothering instinct and ability of a turtle depositing eggs on the beach!"

Dace moved a pace away, as if he didn't trust himself, in his anger, to stay in Kristin's proximity.

"I thought I'd learned a lot from her. But apparently I've been a dunce when it's come to matters of the heart. Of course I suppose that she guided you as I helped my younger brothers and sisters. No doubt she trained you, and believe me, she taught you well. You're such an accomplished actress that I even bought your behavior lock, stock and barrel. I believed you. But, then, I guess all great actresses make the viewers forget where reality ends and fantasy begins. You're the hardworking little maid from Camden Corners?" He gave a scornful, derisive laugh. "What other lies have you told me?"

"I've told you no lies, no lies other than not being able to admit the truth of my sister's identity, for fear that you'd behave exactly as you are reacting right now!"

Dace laughed in her face. "You expect me to believe that? Then you must think me an even bigger, more gullible fool than you and your sister obviously already do."

"I have nothing but respect for you although that's rapidly changing because of the way you won't even let me explain."

"Don't make me laugh. You couldn't ever accomplish that. Not even given all the time remaining in the world."

"I was going to tell you. Tomorrow. Just ask—" She was about to say that Mandy could vouch for her, but then she recalled her promise, and out of loyalty bit the words back.

"Yeah, speaking of her message, why'd she call and leave a message on my machine? She would've known it'd blow things sky high. You two have a regular cat fight? Do something to tick your big sister off, so she took revenge as she could do it best, by revealing you for a fraud to the man you thought you were going to bamboozle into marrying you so you'd have a cushy existence for the rest of your life, and all the money you could spend, whether you stayed married or whether you didn't?"

"I don't know, but I don't need your money, *that* I do know!"

"Oh, what an act it's been," Dace mused, not even seeming to hear her. "And to think I was taken in." His voice was heavy with self-disgust. "I watched you helping Mrs. Moriarty, and thought that I'd found a real lady who could also *work* like a responsible woman, and it made me love you all the more. Now I know that it was just an act, and a necessary evil, so that you could disarm me completely. I'll bet you planned on having a big diamond ring on your finger, and would be intent on putting a ring through my nose before Operation: Recovery could come to a close! Then once we were married, instead of being sweet and understanding and easy to please, you'd revert to true form and not bother to hide your colors. You'd nag, complain, whine, and *demand*: Janice's clone, refusing to lift a finger to do anything, while expecting the staff to behave as if they were your personal servants."

"Get out!" Kristin said. "I've listened to enough of this. To think I was fool enough to think you were nice. Naive enough to fall in love with you. *Get out!*"

"I'll go," Dace said. "But when I'm ready. After all, I do own the place," he pointed out in an unpleasant tone.

"Then *I'll* go!" Kristin raged, the effect diminished somewhat, by the fact that she also burst into tears.

"Good. The sooner the better."

"I'll leave right now."

"I'm sorry, truly sorry, that that's not possible," he pointed out. "For it's the middle of the night. But there's always tomorrow."

And with that he left and slammed the door behind him. He banged it shut with such force that the picture on the wall was knocked askew. The Roving Maid in her dictated that she automatically right it, the way she was helpless to correctly align her life, it seemed. And at the thought Kristin began weeping as she furiously packed her belongings, while knowing that she'd end up leaving her broken heart behind.

Finally, exhausted, she fell into bed.

But still she could not go to sleep.

She felt an odd relief. At last her horrible secret was out. But it had destroyed her world as surely as she'd believed it would.

Dace had been puzzled why Janice had bothered to phone him at his personal residence, at an unlisted number, and leave the message on his machine instead of with the desk help. He'd known that Janice had realized it would provoke a fight, that it would end what had become a pleasant relationship.

Kristin momentarily wondered why Janice had done something so selfish and so cruel. Then, she admitted what she'd always tried to overlook, and she knew the truth beyond denial.

She'd done it because once again Janice was jealous of her little sister, and she didn't want to risk letting Kristin Allen find the happiness that Jan herself constantly sought but never found because she asked too much and offered so little.

Because she had been so mentally exhausted when she'd gone back to bed after packing, and then hadn't been able to sleep until near dawn, Kristin overslept. She hadn't left a wake up call with the desk employees, and when the cries of children at play awoke her, for a moment she thought that she was in her old neighborhood at Camden Corners. Then she looked around, remembered, and with a horrible, sinking heart, recalled every hurtful, insulting, enraged remark Dace had made the evening before. Numb, Kristin arose, showered, put on makeup and tried to make herself presentable.

Her stomach was in such a knot that the thought of food made her feel almost ill.

She wanted nothing more than to get away.

She felt a pang of alarm when she saw the van used to transport people to Rapid City Regional Airport was not there. Determinedly she sought out the driver and made a shaky-voiced inquiry about her chances of going to the airport that day.

"The van's in the shop for an overhaul. We don't do much

scuttling back and forth between the airport and the ranch while the young'uns are here," Roger explained. "So we usually schedule it for a complete overhaul. The mechanic in town picked it up this morning."

"Oh."

"You sound like you're caught between a rock and a hard place."

"Well, I'd hoped to get to the airport to catch a flight."

The cowboy consulted his watch, then shook his head. "A flight leaves in an hour. We couldn't make it. You'd have to be checking it at the gate right now. There's an evening flight, Kristin, and if it's some kind of emergency, I could drive you in my car. I could take off a few hours of personal leave to do it."

"I'd be so grateful. And I'd pay you for your time so you wouldn't lose your wages."

"Before you get your heart set on it, I'd suggest that you go in and call the airline. You know how airlines are these days. The evening flight tends to get cancelled about as often as passengers can fly out."

Back in her room, Kristin made the call, and found out that Roger, who was in a position to know, was right. Her only chance to fly out and away from the Circle K had a departure time minutes away and was booked full.

"There's always tomorrow," she decided, but not with such certainty that she requested passage with the airline for the next day.

Kristin made it a point to leave her room little that day. She unpacked only what she needed. Instead of going to the dining hall, she ate what meals a concerned Mandy brought to her, and when she got hungry, made selections from the coin-operated snack machines near her quarters.

"I wish you'd told him on your own," Mandy commiserated. "I knew that it couldn't help but be so much worse if you let him find out as he did. Your sister is a witch. The type who must make you wish that you had been an only child."

"You can't pick your family, you know," Kristin said in a bleak tone.

"I know it," she said. "Apparently the person who doesn't remember that is Dacian Kendrick."

"He thinks that I'm like Janice. That it's all been an act. And I," Kristin said, "am at the point of not giving a hoot what such an arrogant, opinionated, obstinate, irritating—"

"Hmm. . .as scathing as your remarks, it sounds like you still love him," Mandy sighed teasingly.

Kristin halted. "I suppose that I still do. But believe me, I won't. I'll get over him. You just watch and see. I'm leaving tomorrow."

"Then I guess I won't be able to watch and see, Kris. Because you'll be gone while I'm still here."

"And I'm sure going to miss you."

"It won't seem the same without you."

"You have other friends, Mandy."

"It won't be the same, Kristin."

"I have no choice but to go, the sooner the better. I have to. And now I *want* to." She brushed her hair away from her face. "I don't care if I never see Dacian Kendrick again. . . ."

"That's a lie and we both know it."

"Okay. So it is. But I think I'd rather die than see him face-to-face."

"Don't worry about it, Kris," Mandy said. "No more time than he's spent at the ranch, it's not likely. He's evading you every bit as earnestly as you are zealously avoiding him."

# ten

Kristin was taken by surprise when a quavery voiced, almost tearful Mrs. Moriarty called her room and begged her to come to the housekeeper's quarters as soon as she could.

Not one to turn down a request when someone was upset and in need Kristin put aside what she'd been doing and glanced outside to make sure that Dace was not arriving or departing in his Corvette. She hurried toward the dormitory-like apartment house where Circle K's female staff lived.

Mrs. Moriarty's quarters were on ground level. Her inner door was open although her screen door was closed.

"Knock! Knock!" Kristin called out in a tone much more cheerful than how she felt.

"Come in, child," she invited. "The door's unlocked."

Kristin let herself in and gasped when she saw Mrs. Moriarty, seated in a recliner rocking chair, her right leg elevated, ice packs surrounding it. An accident had swollen it to twice its normal size and colored it an ugly, mottled purple. The skin was stretched tight until Kristin knew how it must throb.

"Oh, how that must hurt," she murmured.

"It's plenty uncomfortable. Although the prescription tablets I've been taking have taken the edge off the pain."

"What happened?"

"I forgot to look where I was going. A child left a baseball bat on the sidewalk. I stepped on it and—"

"It was worse than a banana peel is reputed to be."

"Exactly. Thank goodness I'm no worse than this."

"It could've been a disaster."

"Dr. Bill says I'm lucky that I didn't chip my elbow. Or

135

dislocate a shoulder."

"Or break a hip."

"And I'm no kid anymore," the aging woman remarked.

"Anything I can do to help, Mrs. Moriarty, you just let me know," Kristin said.

"That's why I called you, dear. Dr. Bill says that it's too swollen right now to bother wrapping it. I'm to keep off my feet except when absolutely necessary. And then—" She gestured toward the crutches.

"What rotten luck," Kristin said.

"And it couldn't have happened at a worse time. You know what the children can do to their rooms."

"Oh my. . .I hadn't even thought of what that would mean."

Kristin, who had begun sticking close to her own quarters to avoid Dace until she could manage to leave the ranch, had ceased helping the housekeeping staff. And she'd not gone outside much, staying in her room to the point where she tended to forget that the children were present until something jarringly reminded her.

"I really hate to ask a favor of you, Kristin, because I've heard mumblings around the ranch. I know for a fact that you asked Roger to take you to the Rapid City airport, and that you'd have left us already if you'd been able to get the flight connections arranged. I won't act like I don't know that things are not good between you and Mr. Kendrick, because I believe in telling the truth."

"Well we're not getting along," Kristin said. "And come tomorrow I will be gone."

"Oh no. . . ."

Mrs. Moriarty suddenly looked so worried that Kristin noticed what dark circles had appeared under her eyes, making her look old, feeble, and very, very tired.

"Oh *yes*," Kristin said. "I've already told the staff at the front desk that I'm leaving."

"You can't go, Kristin. I. . .I mean. . .do you have to?"

"I should. I'm not welcome here."

"I think you are. Perhaps not by Dacian. But you are welcome here as far as the other Kendricks are concerned. As for me, all night long as I laid awake, worrying, I kept telling myself that I could stop stewing because you'd be able to help me out. We desperately need you to help out with the housekeeping again."

Kristin's resolve wavered.

She deplored turning her back on someone in need. Especially someone as strong and stoic as Mrs. Moriarty, who would always offer a helping hand quick as a wink, but was hesitant about inconveniencing others by letting her needs be known.

"I'd really like to help you. But I've already given notice I'll be vacating my room."

"It's not likely that there'll be any guests coming in, although I suppose that the staff might have reserved your quarters already. The cowboys who come in for the big rodeo do have to stay someplace. And some of Dace's friends will probably want to get a room here at the ranch." Mrs. Moriarty paused, her face thoughtful. Then she looked up with an expression of last-ditch hope on her pain-filled features. "I'll be sleeping in this chair with my foot elevated," Mrs. Moriarty said. "You can have my bed and bunk here with me. I wouldn't ask such a huge favor of anyone, Kristin, except that I—we—are desperate. There's more work to do, fewer hands to do it, and by the time we could bring some young girls from town and train them to do the housework our way. . .why I'd probably be back on my feet. I've worked with you. You can do the job of two people. I'd see that you were well compensated."

Kristin felt embarrassed. She gave Mrs. Moriarty a pat.

"I know you would," she said. "But the money doesn't matter. It's painful for me to remain here. I don't know what rumors you've heard, but probably anything you've been told is based on the truth. It's hard for me to leave my new friends here. But it would be more of an agony to remain."

"Many things that are painful are the very things that we should do. I'm not just begging you as a helpless old woman, Kristin. I'm also asking on behalf of the children, who really know what pain is all about, and their parents, who are getting a little vacation, too, as we promise to take care of their youngsters as responsibly as we would our own. It's not just me who needs you." Mrs. Moriarty gestured beyond the four walls. "The children do, too."

Kristin forced a smile. "You've just made me an offer that I can't refuse. And I will bunk with you if you don't mind. It'll be good to have some companionship. I've truly missed Mandy now that she's working in Dacian's office."

"That was a wonderful thing you did, Kristin. He's been too overworked, but also too stubborn to admit it. He knows Mandy's a competent girl, or he wouldn't have hired her. He thinks that he did something nice for Mandy and Billy Joe. And he's blind to the fact that he also did something pleasant for himself. He needs to relax more."

"Sometimes he seems so. . .driven."

"I think he is. Dacian Kendrick is a very complex man." She paused. "He was a very complex little boy. So serious. So solemn. And always so responsible." Her voice dropped off to become low musings that seemed almost more to herself than to Kristin. "I hate to think where I'd be without Dacian Kendrick as my boss."

Kristin sighed inwardly. More testimonials were not exactly what she wanted to hear, as needled as she felt by the wonderful Mr. Kendrick who'd so cruelly railed at her.

"Dacian was just a lad when my Harley was wounded in a rodeo accident. He didn't die right away. He lingered for a week, and it was awful. My heart broke by inches and degrees every day that he lingered. And the bills, of course, mounted higher and higher."

"That's so sad. It must've been hard."

"It'd have been a lot harder. I managed to hang onto my ranch, but it wasn't easy. About that time Dacian came into his own and began this dude ranch, employing his brothers and sisters, but making sure that each of them went to college, while he, himself, took night classes in the evenings and kept the enterprise going during the day. When he slept, I'll never know."

"I know he's an accomplished man," Kristin admitted.

"Running the ranch was becoming too much for me. One day Dace Kendrick drove in, a handsome young cowboy who'd turn any woman's head. He offered to buy my ranch that adjoins this spread. Knowing my need, many a man would've dickered for the lowest dollar amount possible. Not Dace Kendrick. He knew how hard it was when his father died, only a few years after they'd lost his brother. If anything he offered me more than my ranch was worth."

"That's really admirable."

"I needed to sell. I wanted to sell. But I truly hated to leave the area where I'd lived all of my life. People are like trees. They set down roots. Rip 'em up, and so often they wither and die. Dace knows that about folks, especially us ranchers. And he told me that he wanted to expand the ranch. But to do it, he'd have to have people he could count on. He allowed as to how he knew that I could be the best manager of the housekeeping staff that he could ask for. And," she said, as pride came into her voice, "I like to think I've never let that boy down."

"I'm sure you haven't."

"I hope I haven't. Because he's been like a son to me, and I don't think I could love him more if I were his mother." She paused. "And it's because I do love that boy that I want to see him happy. You made him happy, Kristin. Now you've made him sad. Or so he thinks. I not only need you to stick around to help us with all of the housework. I'd like you to remain here until that bullheaded young pup comes to his senses and recognizes that you're the woman meant for him. The God-sent woman who'll give him lifelong joy."

Kristin couldn't help the bitter laugh that erupted.

"I'm afraid I must beg to disagree; he made it perfectly clear that he'd be happy if he never laid eyes on me again."

Mrs. Moriarty made a piffling gesture. "What a man says and what he really thinks are often not one and the same. Just because Dace Kendrick rages it does not mean that you're required to believe it."

"He was very convincing." Kristin wiped her eyes. "I never want to see him again. I've felt like a prisoner in my room, afraid that we'd accidentally meet on the sidewalk somewhere."

"Well, you won't have to worry about seeing him if you stay on. When you're not cleaning rooms, you can hole up here. They can bring your meals along with mine. And Dr. Bill won't say anything about your being here. From what I've seen, and the girls tell me, Dacian is making himself scarce. That convinces me that he still feels something for you, Kristin, or he wouldn't stay away. The reason he's not showing hide nor hair is because he's afraid to. Frightened that what he feels will be so strong and true that he'll end up taking back everything he said, and having to swallow that pride of his and say that he's sorry."

"Which certainly wouldn't hurt him. But what about his family? I haven't seen any of them. I figured that people would be taking sides. And they are his immediate family. So I'd assumed—"

"It was Dr. Bill who suggested that you might help out again. And he won't tell Dace, I'm sure, because right now he and Dace aren't on the best of terms. Nor is he with Melly. Or Kerry. I would suppose he feels betrayed that they've taken your side instead of his."

"Th. . .they still like me? And believe in me?"

Mrs. Moriarty nodded. "They think you're super, Kris, and just the woman for a man like Dace Kendrick, the big boss of the Circle K Spread. They're really hoping that you two will sort out your differences, and that Dace will give you the Kendrick family ring, that by tradition goes to the wife of the oldest son, and claim you for his own."

Kristin's thoughts were swirling.

As she'd listened to Mrs. Moriarty, she remembered so many good things about Dace that it made it easier to overlook his rare forays into unpleasantness.

Although she'd wanted to leave, she now felt drawn to staying, but she could not admit it, not to Mrs. Moriarty, because she wasn't comfortable acknowledging it herself. . . .

"I'll stay," Kristin quietly agreed. "But only for a few days. And for the children's sake. We do have an obligation to them and their parents."

"A few days is all we ask, Kristin, and pray God that's all that's required for Dace to bury his anger, find his good sense, and settle this matter once and for all by realizing that you can't judge a book by its cover, nor decide what one girl's like because you've previously met her sister."

For the next two days Kristin's daytime hours were spent slipping from building to building, working quietly, scrubbing, dusting, vacuuming, and bringing order to the children's chaos.

She talked with the young ranch guests who had to take naps and rest more than other children did. She found them loving, funny, earnest and so sweet that her heart wrenched when she feared she'd never know what it was like to have a child of her own.

As the days progressed she was relieved when Dace's parking slot remained vacant, because it meant that she wouldn't have to worry about walking out of a building, her cleaning cart rolling along in front of her, and come face-to-face with him.

By the time she'd remained for three days, she really wanted to leave. It was torment being so close to Dacian by geography, yet so far apart emotionally that he could've been around the world. But her rashly given promise in the face of Mrs. Moriarty's almost coercive pleading was a vow she couldn't break. The elderly woman worried enough as it was, and if Kristin left, she knew that it was all too likely Mrs. Moriarty would begin putting weight on her badly sprained ankle, before Dr. Bill said that it was all right for her to be up and about. That could result in a broken hip, which so often meant the end of good health to older people.

Because she felt a bit uncomfortable, Kristin tried to be away from Mrs. Moriarty's quarters when Dr. Bill Kendrick was due to arrive to check her ankle.

He confronted her when he arrived unexpectedly and caught her sitting with Mrs. Moriarty.

"Can we talk?" he asked.

"Sure," she said, with a casual calm she didn't really feel.

"Let's take a little stroll," he suggested. Wordlessly Kristin followed him outside. "Dace is still in a snit. The rest of us don't agree with him. But, unfortunately, his view is the one that matters to you," he said and eased his glasses up, rubbing the bridge of his nose in a tired gesture. "None of us can change his mind. We've tried. Believe me we've tried."

"I don't know if I appreciate it or not."

Dr. Bill gave a small smile. "I'm not here hinting for thanks, but to extend it, Kristin. We're very grateful to you. I know that the children think you're tops. I'm sure it's not been easy to always give a child a smiling face when inside you feel like crying."

"You're right. And I'll be glad when Mrs. Moriarty is back on her feet so I can go home with a clear conscience."

"It'll be soon, Kristin. Just a matter of a few days. Think you can hang in there for that long?"

"It won't be easy," she admitted. "But I'll try."

"You've been working so hard," Dr. Bill observed. "And by the looks of you there's a strong chance that you're not eating as you should. Appetite dwindling?" She nodded. "Not unusual when a person is upset. Just do your best. You should try to relax; do something fun."

"You're a great one to give me such advice, Doctor," she said. "I've seen you working almost 'round the clock."

"The cobbler's children do without shoes, and the doctor often ignores his best bits of advice."

"I do get bored staying inside all the time, but it's difficult to be around people, adults, who know Dace, are employed by him, and who he might think are disloyal if—"

"Surely he's not that unreasonable."

"Isn't he? Anyway, I don't want to make use of what facilities the ranch offers for fear that Dacian will return, and he'll see me, and in anger force another confrontation. Thinking that I'm hanging around to be a thorn in his side instead of as a favor to others."

"But couldn't you go for a ride? The pastures are quite private. And the bluffs and plateaus are nice. Serene. Especially in the evening when the children aren't stampeding all over the hills, whooping and shrieking and playing cowboys and Indians. Why don't you start taking a ride each evening?"

"I'll think about it," Kristin said, realizing that the idea appealed to her more than a little.

"Then consider it doctor's orders," Bill said and gave her a grin so much like Dace's during happier times, that she turned away, feeling as if her heart was breaking anew.

That night after taking her meal with Mrs. Moriarty and visiting a bit with Mandy when she came to Mrs. Moriarty's quarters, Kristin felt oddly restless.

She didn't feel like watching television, nor did she want to risk an encounter with Dace by going to the large building where children were square dancing to rollicking tunes that could be heard far away from the dance floor.

Kristin had closed her eyes and was listening to the bouncy tunes, when she realized that she detected a different rhythm at counterpoint with the fiddle's lilting beat.

It took her a moment to realize that it was the steady *clip clop* of horses.

"Whoa. . . ." she heard a soft voice outside her door command.

Kristin sat up, then went to the door and glanced out. Dace's younger sister, who was a third year nursing student, was astride a roan that she tended to select for her mount, and she was leading Molly alongside. The plump mare was saddled up and ready to go.

"Let's go for a ride, Kristin," Melanie said, swinging down. "And I won't take no for an answer," she warned before Kristin could open her mouth. "It'll do you good."

Molly lifted her head, revealed flat, wide, yellowed horse teeth, laid back her ears, looked as if she were smiling, and issued a low nicker.

Melanie slapped her jean clad thigh and laughed.

"Hear that? We're going for a ride at the special invitation of Miss Molly herself. Even if you thought about turning me down, you *can't* decline an offer like that."

"I guess not," Kristin said, laughing, and suddenly felt at ease with Dace's younger sister. "Let me slip on a pair of boots and grab a jacket and I'll be right with you."

She rejoined Melly moments later after telling Mrs. Moriarty where she was going.

As Kristin took the reins, Molly gave her an affectionate nuzzle, snuffling at the back of her jacket, and blowing out her breath in an impatient snort, with the moist gust of air tickling Kristin's skin.

"Now behave yourself, Molly!" Kristin ordered. "We all know that you have a reputation to live up to."

She stuck her left foot in the stirrup, shoved off with her

right foot, and swung her leg over, settling into the saddle. She gave Molly a pat.

"The greeting you gave me, old girl, Mandy will be jealous. So would your owner," she said, "whoever he or she is. I'll bet whoever owns you will be glad to have such a sweet old horse return after the children have gone home."

Melly gave Kristin a rather startled look, seemed about to say something, but then apparently thought better of it and did not. The two women slowly rode along the wide street then out into the vast expanses beneath the twilight South Dakota sky.

At first Kristin felt self-conscious, being with the sister of the man she still loved, while she, and every adult on the Circle K, had been made aware that Dacian despised her.

But gradually talk between them became easier.

"Kristin, can I ask you something?"

"I suppose."

"I won't if you think I have no right to get a bit personal."

"If I think you're too personal, I don't have to answer," Kristin replied.

"That's fair enough. So I may's well cut right to the heart of the matter. Are you going to try to get Dacian back?"

"Why do you ask?" Kristin responded to Melly's question by asking one of her own.

"Because we're hoping that you will. And if there's anything that we can do to help, let us know. We care about Dace, but we've also come to care for you. He's not a totally happy man. Dace isn't fit for man nor beast to be around these days. And now, instead of feeling like he's settled the issue, it's as if he's in a worse fettle because while he's done what he wanted to do, and hurt you the way he couldn't wound your sister, deep down he knows he's like the man who cut off his nose to spite his face."

"Sorry to disappoint you. And I can appreciate your concern and sentiments, but the answer is no. I haven't any plans to try to get him back. And I'd appreciate it if you wouldn't do anything to intervene. It could end up making things worse. And of course Dacian would blame me."

"You're probably right," Melanie said in a bleak tone. "We all hate to see you both so unhappy."

"I'll be all right. Don't worry about me. I'll be fine just as soon as we have Mrs. Moriarty get back back on her feet so I can go."

Melly seemed to think it over. "Well, never forget that the rest of us are your friends, Kristin, and if you're ever passing through areas where any of us live, we'll be disappointed if you don't stop in to visit."

"I'd like that," Kristin said. "And it's reassuring to know that not everyone thinks I'm an awful person because my sister seems to be."

"I'm glad you're not prejudiced against me because of how my big brother's treating you."

Kristin started to say something, but then their attention was drawn to a rider who was coming across the pasture with his horse going at full gallop.

"That's Tony!" Melanie said. "I'd better go see what he wants. It was his sister's due date today, maybe he's going to tell me that he's just become an uncle. Want to ride back to headquarters with us? Or continue on your ride?"

"I think I'll go it alone, thanks," she said. "The night's still young. And this is the most peaceful I've felt all week."

"Remember, you're on Molly," Melanie warned. "I guess you've heard about her and what she does if she thinks you're not an expert enough rider to show her who's boss."

"I think we'll get along fine."

"Well she can be a handful. And we're not too far from where her owner lives. Keep a firm rein, because she can be as headstrong as she is lovable. A lot like her owner, I guess."

"I'll be all right. Don't worry. I can take care of myself."

As dusk began to drape over the ranch in the rapidly fading light, Kristin looked for familiar paths. She seemed to remember some of them, but about the time she believed she was on the way home, she'd confront a landmark she'd never seen before, and soon her confusion was complete.

For the better part of an hour she'd let Molly mosey along wherever she chose, and now she regretted it, for the horse was determined to go where she wanted, not where Kristin desired.

"Well, you stubborn old hayburner," Kristin said, "then I guess we'll just go where you want to, and when I meet your master I'm going to apologize and tell him what you did and ask him if he'll give me a ride back to the Circle K. With any luck he'll be able to deliver me right to Mrs. Moriarty's doorstep."

As the darkness began to descend in earnest, she felt a prickle of alarm. But when the sky grew dark enough, before the moon rose, she saw lights from a house glowing on the adjoining ranch.

When she and Molly climbed a bluff and Kristin was at a vantage point so that she could look out over the area, she saw what had to be myriad lights from the Circle K glowing off in the distance, and she turned Molly in that direction, determined to show the stubborn creature who was boss.

But the chunky horse had other ideas. Molly snorted, stomped, threw her head back, and even threatened to rear.

"Stop it!" Kristin cried, and there was fright in her voice, that Molly probably heard, so she knew that Kristin's order was a command that she need not heed.

At last Molly started to move. Sighing with relief, Kristin thought that they were heading back in the direction of the Circle K, until a moment later when she understood that Molly had taken a shortcut, and the wily mare had instead progressed toward the ranch where only a few lights glowed in the night.

When the mare increased her pace, Kristin realized that Molly's excitement indicated that she was just about home!

Mentally Kristin rehearsed her embarrassed explanations.

She'd tell the kindly ranch owner, who of course already knew what Molly was like, that she'd been riding the horse, thought she was competent, but found that she wasn't the match for one lovable but stubborn horse.

Molly seemed to know her way around, and with brisk movements, so frisky that Kristin had to hang onto the pommel to keep from being thrown off in the darkness, Molly negotiated the dark terrain.

"Oh, no!" Kristin cried in horror when Molly went through an open gate, entered a large yard, then went to stand expectantly at a stable gate. It was not just any stable gate, but the stable gate on *Dacian Kendrick's private property!*

Molly was home. . . .

With a nicker that shattered the still night, she began to make almost mule-like brays. The evening was pleasant, Dace's windows were open, and within a moment he was outside to investigate.

"Who's out there?" he called.

Molly gave a delighted nicker and trotted over to see him as if she were thrilled to at last lay eyes on him. Shameless as a hussy she nuzzled him while Kristin cowered in the shadows.

Dace touched the saddle, and seemed to know from the leather's warmth that it had been unseated mere moments before.

"Whoever you are, you'd better come out. Don't be alarmed. This is Molly's oldest trick. I'll see you back to the Circle K. And remind the staff at the corral not to give Molly to a novice again."

Kristin didn't answer. She was frozen with horror, beyond the capacity to produce speech.

"Come on, kiddo," Dacian said, his tone having a hint of exasperation. "I'm not going to call your mom and dad and tell on you. You're not in trouble, so be a pal and come out. Okay?"

Still Kristin didn't answer.

She heard Dace mutter under his breath to Molly, then he went into the house while Molly patiently waited. He returned with a powerful lantern. He easily swung into the saddle, jerked Molly around, and she knew better than to disobey *him*.

She started to canter past where Kristin was standing, but the horse sensed her and shied. In the process the all-around cowboy was almost thrown over her head. He flicked on the lantern as he jerked on the reins, making Molly rear, as her front hooves lashed the air not far from Kristin's face.

"Who's there?" he cried out.

Dace swung the light around, and the beam crisscrossed the nearby lawn. Then it came to focus on Kristin's face, blinding her. The look he gave her was beyond description. In the glow of the lantern that reflected up toward his face, she was certain that even in the dim light she saw his complexion drain.

"*You!*" he said. His tone was stunned, disbelieving, as if he couldn't comprehend that she was standing on his property. "What are you doing here?" Startled, miserable, Kristin couldn't answer, except for an awkward, defiant shrug. "Don't bother to explain, I'm sure that I know exactly what you're here for. Been talking to big sister, have you? Has she been offering tutelage? Advising you how to get a man back? Well, my dear girl, *it won't work.*"

"That isn't what I had in mind," Kristin said. "I wouldn't have you if you were the last man on earth. You're the most unpleasant man on the face of the earth."

"And you, my dear, are tied for first place, as one of the most devious women I have ever met."

Dacian was poised to say more.

But Kristin decided that she didn't have to listen and wouldn't. With steps that were heavy because of her tough leather riding boots, she sprinted for the pasture and the bushes and shrubs and trees beyond. She was panting for breath as she raced through the darkness, intent on finding cover before Dacian Kendrick could reach her.

"Kristin!" he yelled as he guided Molly around, flashing the lantern here and there, hunting. "Would you come out? This isn't funny. Don't you realize that I'm responsible for you? You're on ranch property."

Kristin pinched her lips shut and said not a word.

"Kristin, please. You don't know your way around. There are animals. And you shouldn't be stumbling around in the dark among the rattlesnakes. Be a good girl, you little fool, and I'll take you home."

For a moment Kristin was tempted.

But then she decided she'd rather take her chances with the snakes.

She cowered in the bushes until Dace returned to his house after putting a triumphantly nickering Molly back in her paddock.

Then he roared away in his Corvette.

Kristin got up, stretching the kinks out of her spine. She looked at Molly, silhouetted in the moonlight, and she was tempted to saddle her up and strike out for the Circle K.

Two things stopped her.

One, Molly probably wouldn't go.

And two, it would provide Dacian Kendrick the right to add "horse thief" to her lengthening list of supposed transgressions.

Grimly Kristin faced toward the lights glaring into the sky to the north, and started out walking, step by careful step.

With any luck, she'd be home by dawn.

# eleven

Minutes after Dace's Corvette shot down his driveway toward the main road, Kristin started walking, intent on putting distance between them before he could return to hunt her down and shepherd her back to the Circle K ranch like a wayward, incompetent child.

The first few minutes after she'd stepped from the perimeter of Dace's immaculately tended lawn and into the increasingly tangled wilds of the vast pastureland, she was in misery.

Every time a twig snapped, an insect rasped, an owl hooted, a coyote yipped, or a dust devil riffled through the prairie grass, causing it to crackle and saw around her legs, she almost jumped out of her skin. She gasped with alarm, whimpering, when she considered rattlesnakes and other unseen threats hidden by the night.

At the thought of a thick-bodied, diamond-backed reptile silently slithering toward her, forked tongue flitting, rattles whirring a warning, her heart pounded with fright, and spurts of adrenaline shot into her system, causing her fingertips to tingle from the effect.

But then she thought about how God was sovereign over His Creation, how He had dominion over all. That He knew when a sparrow fell and the exact number of hairs on her head. Everything was in the Lord's control and no evil would touch her unless the Lord allowed the event to take place in order that He might work good with it one day. There was nothing for her to fear, and she prayed for God to give her relief from the fright she felt welling inside, threatening to erupt with just the right squirmy, startling nocturnal catalyst.

It was enough to make her plaintively cry out for Dace, to beg him to come rescue her, except that he'd already departed as if she were not worth the effort. She'd chosen her course of action, now she had no alternative but follow it through until she arrived back at the ranch under her own power.

Kristin sighed, halted to get her bearings, then stood, resolute, as she mentally mapped out her strategy. She had a long hike ahead of her, and it would become an almost unbearable ordeal if she attempted it in a state of near hysteria.

"Stop it," she muttered to herself, as she tried to convince herself that she had nothing to fear but her own self-induced terrors. She prayed for God to give her courage and serenity.

Instead it seemed to her that she began to recall what Dace had told her about animals in the wild, how they didn't threaten humans unless they felt threatened themselves or were protecting their young. She realized that they, even snakes, would hurry from her approach, and that her chances of a startling confrontation were almost nil.

Plus, she was well-equipped for the walk back to the woods. She had on almost knee-high tough leather riding books, and her rugged denim jeans were tucked down inside. She had a denim jacket against the evening chill and even a small portable spray can of mosquito repellent in her pocket.

Suddenly she felt competent; prepared to cope with almost anything. Or anyone. Except Dace Kendrick.

She suddenly realized that he hadn't just stormed away from his ranch, roaring over the roads in the Corvette because he was piqued with her, but because he was worried and was no doubt at the Circle K Ranch right at that moment, organizing a search party of men on horseback and perhaps even on all-terrain vehicles.

She shuddered at the thought. Her humiliation wouldn't be a matter between her and Dace, it would become public record, and probably the talk of the ranch, as workers would be routed from their beds and ordered to go in search of the woman Dace despised, even as he accepted responsibility for her safety.

She'd begun to consider herself an accomplished enough horsewoman, by city slicker standards, and she felt a flush of embarrassment that she'd been bested by a wily old mare, who was as headstrong and singleminded as her owner.

And how shocked she had been to learn that the anonymous ranch owner, the person who shipped the lovable old mare to the Circle K Ranch each summer for a month's use and who lived on an adjoining spread, was none other than Dace Kendrick.

Gradually the facts began to sift through Kristin's mind, and as if she were sorting out data, mentally stacking it in piles, then assembling it in chronological order, she saw the pattern emerge.

And with a startled gasp she realized that she'd been hoodwinked by Dacian's family, just as surely as she'd been outfoxed by that plump, stubborn horse. When she'd given Molly her head, she thought the mare was going to obey and head back to the Circle K, only to realize too late that Molly had taken an alternative route back to the owner she adored.

Kristin had always heard that an individual could fool another person, but that it was impossible to deceive an animal.

At the moment, Kristin thought that Dace was the most impossible man on earth. But obviously Molly thought he was the most wonderful.

"I've heard of horse sense," Kristin mused to herself. "What if she's right?"

Then she realized that both she and Molly were right.

Kristin had to honestly tote up Dace's many wonderful traits, personality aspects that, of course, would cause the old horse he'd probably had since he was a youth to adore him.

Then she every bit as honestly noted his flaws, as if they were jotted in a column in her mind.

While the good traits were many, and the flaws were few, she found no comfort in the fact, for the differences that parted them were so serious as to make her all but forget the wonderful moments that they had shared—funny events, tender interludes, heartfelt talks of Christian faith. Kristin's beliefs had solidified and strengthen after Mrs. Stanwyck had helped her to come to know the Lord, and contact with Mandy, Dace, Billy Joe and others had all had an edifying effect. It was as if all these things were overcome by hurtful memories that had begun compiling since the first moment that they had officially met.

Kristin made steady progress as she strode through the night and reflected on what had taken place. Gradually as she adjusted to the nocturnal sounds, in the same way her eyes grew accustomed to the dark, she began to feel as if she were one with the night. Oddly enough Kristin had never felt closer to God, nor more protected by Him, her destiny in His loving care.

Kristin realized that she had to have been heading in a northerly direction for at least the better part of an hour, maybe even more, although it was hard to accurately judge time, as preoccupied as she'd become. It was still too dark to read the face of her watch. To the east a summer moon was rising, pale and coldly white, to cast a thin silvery sheen over the landscape, shedding enough light to inkily outline objects now that her eyes had grown accustomed to the total dark surrounding her like soft black velet.

Far away to the north, like a welcoming beacon in a sea of darkness, the outdoor lights of the Circle K Ranch glowed a steady signal marking her way through the night.

Trying to put the situation with Dace from mind, Kristin considered what she knew about South Dakota, the wild land she'd come to love, that was as diverse as the people who had settled it.

Bathed in moonlight, she had an appreciation for the time-lessness of the land upon which she walked. She thought of the prehistoric animals whose fossils could be found preserved in rocks, with their presence revealed by the steady, eternal flow of water, the force eventually unearthing ancient history to mankind who mastered the land at the moment, marveling at their Creator's timeless touch.

She felt a sudden empathy with the pioneers, Dace's ancestors he'd spoken of, who'd stood on the land, perhaps venturing across the terrain beneath the moon's guiding light because it had been too hot for the women, children, and animals to trek on in Conestogas during the daytime summer hours. Then to proceed west a few more miles, a journey that had probably taken days, only to confront lands so bad, the Bad-lands, that in despair they'd turned back to settle on grounds more hospitable.

She considered Dace's ancestors and had an idea of the kind of people they'd been, judging by the legacy they'd passed down through the years.

Doubtless, they were a people who didn't give up. When they wanted something, they went after it. And if at first they didn't succeed, they picked themselves up, dusted off, and tried again, having faith in a good outcome. Knowing that with the Lord, joy would follow sorrow, laughter would come in the wake of tears, fulfillment after a time of disappoint-ment, trials and tribulations that God had allowed that it might make straighter the journey of faith that led to peace everlast-ing.

That is, except where she was concerned. It was unlikely that Dacian Kendrick would ever give her a second chance.

Her steps drew to an abrupt stop and she almost toppled with surprise. Instead, wearily sinking to a boulder that still retained the afternoon sun's blazing heat, she realized that she'd not only been tricked by Molly, but she'd been bested by Melanie and Dr. Bill as well. They'd used the old horse as their most willing conspirator to force her to a confrontation with Dace in hopes that instead of both of them retreating into hurt and disillusionment, they would actually communicate, allowing their mutual interests and shared faith to draw them together for a united walk through life.

Kristin couldn't help uttering a weak laugh when she looked back and with good old twenty-twenty hindsight, saw with such clarity what had not been obvious until a moment before.

She remembered Dr. Bill's questions, his concerns, and how he'd tried to plead Dace's case and explain his brother to a woman who'd already come to know him so well and to understand him, on down to his occasional fits of irrational unreasonableness.

"'Doctor's orders,' indeed!" Kristin muttered, sniffing, and idly wondered if she should jokingly tease Bill about considering a malpractice suit for so idly tinkering with matters of the heart, reminding him that a physician was to do a patient no harm.

But, then, he hadn't, she realized. Dr. Bill Kendrick, as the excellent physician that he was, had simply been trying to promote the healing of a relationship, prescribing the only treatment that he saw as having a chance at working a miracle cure.

And Melanie had been a most cooperative nurse practitioner!

Kristin had promised Dr. Bill that she'd consider starting to take rides in the evening. But in truth she knew that that's as far as she'd have taken the matter, mere consideration. She wouldn't have proceeded as far as direct action.

So Melanie, like a nurse bearing an antidote, had, on doctor's orders appeared on Kristin's doorstep, prepared to see to it that Kristin took her treatments, administering a 'dose of Molly,' knowing it would take effect quickly.

It hadn't been happenstance that Melanie had selected Molly for Kristin, she realized. And it hadn't been an accident that they'd ridden out in the direction they had. Nor, Kristin realized, had it been a matter of fate that Tony had come riding out looking for Melanie. For the pretty woman's fiance was surely but another name to add to the list of conspirators.

No doubt they had hoped to force a confrontation and had believed that if Kristin and Dace would just face one another, talk like adults, and with initial fiery angers cooled, *communicate*, the problems and misunderstandings would be resolved. They had hoped for peace and unity for the people at the Circle K Ranch who had been caught in the unpleasant situation of being expected to take sides by the headstrong man and the sensitive woman pitted against one another.

Momentarily, she felt a twinge of regret that she had turned tail and run away from Dace, instead of boldly facing him, *making* him listen to her as it was now so apparent others wanted her to do.

And, as she arose from the boulder and continued walking, a small part of her wondered if he would've listened to her.

She would never forget the expressions that had washed across his face, evolving like shapes in a kalideoscope, as one emotion gave way to another, seeming to convey everything on the spectrum in a split second.

She'd seen concern when he'd believed Molly had accomplished what would have been nothing short of an equine kidnapping.

She'd seen relief when he'd located Molly's rider, unhurt.

His look had then become shock when he'd focused and recognized the features of Molly's hostage as *her*.

That brief expression had merged with a look that had momentarily sent Kristin's heart soaring, because it had been a fleeting glimpse of what looked like tender, relieved love, before it was quickly and determinedly replaced by a look of angry contempt, and he'd begun flinging accusations about her actions based on his experiences with her sister.

But what haunted her was that when she had confronted him face-to-face, he'd almost looked overjoyed at seeing her until he forcibly reminded himself that she was a woman he did not like and could not trust. No doubt he believed her professions of a shared faith in Christ a sham, not a maturing way of life and belief. It was that look that had caused Kristin to turn on her heel and run into the night.

And without glancing back, without having to, she knew that the look cast in her direction had then become one of utter exasperation that she'd fled from him, obviously willing to take her chances with snakes rather than remain another moment with him.

The moon was directly overhead when Kristin topped a bluff. She paused to catch her breath after making the uphill climb and was quite certain that she was halfway back to the Circle K Ranch. Although she'd made good time, it was still a long walk ahead of her.

When she saw lights in the distance, roving, jerking about, panning across the terrain, flitting into the sky, she realized that Dace had routed out employees and they had fanned out on the all-terrain vehicles possessed by the Circle K to be used to haul feed, save steps in doing necessary chores, and search for lost riders as they were now doing for her.

Kristin kept walking. The small but rough and durable little vehicles were noisy enough so that she could hear their approach well in advance as they drew near her, and she could take evasive actions. She wanted to walk back under her own, not be taken back, feeling like a recalcitrant child forced to surrender.

Kristin hadn't traveled moved more than an additional quarter of a mile before she heard unfamiliar sounds in the dark, coming from behind her. She'd been so intent on monitoring the progress of the search party on the vehicles ahead of her that she hadn't stopped to consider that there was also a search party closing in from behind.

She stood stock still, listening.

Men on horseback! And their positions would be hard to reconoiter because they were letting their horses pick and choose their way, their eyes as accustomed to the light as Kristin's had become, so that they conserved their flashlight batteries and only flicked their lanterns on when they investigated shapes in the pasture.

Kristin, although she was tired, didn't want to be caught and treated like a disobedient child, especially by Dace, who she sensed was one of the riders who'd mounted up after they'd obviously transported horses by van to his spread to begin a search from that direction.

Quickly, panting from the exertion and tension, her hair whipping back and forth as she scanned the immediate vicinity for a hiding place, she moved toward a large area where brambles, briars, and scruffy brush formed an almost impenetrable thicket. To save face she had no choice but to wedge herself into the underbrush, biting her lip to hold back cries of pain as thorns raked at her exposed skin and tangled in her hair, harshly tugging it every time she moved a bit to burrow deeper and wait for the riders to pass by.

"If she's come this way," Dace said in a tired voice, "she must be part Indian, because she's moved through with the grace and finesse of a warrior."

"My thoughts exactly," another rider, who Kristin recognized as Billy Joe, agreed.

"Let's pause a moment to let the horses rest," Dace suggested.

The saddle leathers creaked as the two dismounted.

Kristin frowned and gave an almost inaudible sigh over the fact that they'd accidentally selected the location where she'd hidden herself to confer before they moved out again.

Or was it simply another one of Dace's tricks? Did they know *exactly* where she was? And Dace was toying with her, as he'd probably done with the information being compiled by the private investigator, before Janice's telephone call had presented incontrovertible evidence to confront her with?

The horses stood so close to her that she could hardly breathe for the musky, sweaty odors as they stomped, steadily swished their coarse tails at flies, and huffed and snorted with impatience.

"Well, we'd better mount up again," Dace said. "Perhaps she hasn't come this far from my spread. But she's a plucky woman, and determined. . ."

"Not to mention probably very angry," Billy Joe softly added. "Mandy's going to be an unhappy woman if we don't find her friend. She wasn't happy that Kristin was given Molly, being as Mandy herself was constantly warned about your old horse."

"It was a trick," Dace said, confirming Kristin's suspicions.

"A trick?"

"Compliments of the Kendrick family. It appears that Melly went to the corral and selected two horses. When she picked out Molly, she was reminded that she wasn't to leave the corrals. And you know how Melanie can be. Sweet as could be she told the ranch hand in charge to mind his own business, that she knew exactly what she was doing."

Billy Joe began to laugh. "And I reckon she did. It was one way to see to it that you and Kristin started talkin' again."

"But we didn't. Why, I'd hardly opened my mouth before she turned tail and ran."

"Hardly opened your mouth?" Billy Joe echoed, his slightly mocking disbelief evident in his tone.

Dace sighed, the sound cutting through the darkness to reach Kristin. "Okay, so I said things I shouldn't have."

"Again?" Billy Joe said softly.

"*Again*," Dace admitted heavily. "And if I don't want to keep doing this to Kristin, I have to get to the bottom of my anger. Tomorrow, when all this is over and I know Kris is safe, I'm making an appointment to talk with Pastor Johnson and get some counseling."

"We'd better start looking for her," Billy Joe said. "Obviously the guys on the ATVs haven't had any luck finding her."

"I don't now how I'll ever forgive myself if something has happened to her," Dacian murmured. Kristin felt her heart melt when she detected the tender concern in his voice that seemed to transcend the emotions he'd feel for just any ranch guest who was lost. "I love her, even though a part of me hasn't wanted to. . . ."

"Aw, I'll bet she's okay. Maybe sittin' on a rock somewhere waiting to be rescued."

"I wish we'd find her. Although I don't know what I'd ever say to her."

Billy Joe made an impatient sound of incredulousness. "Why don't you try starting off with 'I'm sorry'?"

"A good idea," Dace said.

"And then you could get real brave and follow it up with, 'I love you. . . .' I know how you feel, God knows, but does she?"

"An even better suggestion," Dace said. "And I really do love her, you know."

"Yeah, I know, Boss," Billy Joe said and gave a laugh. "Along with everyone else on the Circle K. The only one who doesn't know how you feel about her now is Kristin. And you, before you came to your senses. You now realize it. So convince Kristin."

"Let's move out," Dace softly ordered. "I've got to find her and attend to some personal business."

For a moment Kristin had been tempted to wriggle from her hiding place, revealing herself to them as she'd probably risk spooking their horses. But then she stayed where she was, realizing that she wasn't quite ready to surrender yet. She wanted, instead, to walk through the silent night, treasuring in her heart the things she'd overheard Dace confide to Billy Joe Blaylock.

By the time she'd walked back to the Circle K, perhaps she would know her own heart, and have it finalized in her mind just exactly how to deal with the upcoming confrontation that she knew she was destined to have with Dace Kendrick, the big boss of the Circle K Ranch, who could but with the right words become the sole owner of her trusting woman's heart.

When enough time passed, Kristin decided that the riders must have given up and called off any further search until daylight.

Kristin found that her steps seemed to slow as she neared the headquarters, and she recognized her own reluctance to face Dace. She wouldn't be able to bear it if instead of expressing relief, he thundered at her out of the grateful emotion that she wasn't hurt and had scared him so badly that he momentarily lost control again.

As dawn approached, the sky began to lighten as the moon started to sink into the western sky, although the sun had not begun to appear over the horizon.

Able to see much better in the dim morning light, Kristin looked across the hazy pasture and realized that she wasn't very far from the headquarters. When the sky brightened as morning drew nigh, the dusk-to-dawn utility lights that made the Circle K glow like a diamond against the black sky and had served as a beacon to her disappeared.

She glanced at her watch. It was four-thirty in the morning, and she considered what was probably going on at the ranch. The riders who'd been out during the night were probably in the dining hall eating a hearty breakfast, drinking down cups of strong black coffee to shake away their weariness and fuel them to begin another search for her once daylight arrived.

She hurried her steps, wanting to reach the ranch before she could inconvenience them anymore.

As she topped a rise and looked down upon the Circle K headquarters, she thought she'd never seen such a glorious sight, for at that moment the sun had swiftly risen and had cast a fiery glow over the side of one of the buildings that served as children's quarters.

She paused to enjoy the serene moment when suddenly she realized that the orange glow wasn't the sun's reflection. She glanced to the east and discovered to her horror that the sun hadn't arisen yet, and the horizon was showing only the shelly pink promise of a beautiful day.

"No!" Kristin shrieked.

Adrenaline shot through her system again, giving her the swiftness and strength that she'd never have dreamed she could've mustered as her numb legs picked up speed and her boots pounded over the rough terrain. She screamed warnings with every gasping breath she took.

"Fire!" she cried. "*FIRE!*"

Couldn't they hear her? she wondered, almost sobbing in frustration. She increased her speed, almost tripping over her own feet as forward momentum increased.

And the children! Couldn't they feel the heat? Smell the smoke? At the thought of them burning in their beds, or suffocating, dying from smoke inhalation, their parents stunned and shocked beyond coping, with a guilty Dace Kendrick forever buried beneath a mantle of crushing unmet responsibility that would ruin what days remained in his life, Kristin found the reserves to run even faster.

She leaped over low thickets of rough grass, dodged prairie dog holes and thudded on. Her legs felt as if they were lead, and her ribs stabbed her lungs with every breath. She had a stitch in her side that almost made her cry out with the intensity if she hadn't been screaming warnings to those below. They were either sleeping so soundly that they did not hear or were listening to the morning farm forecasts on the radio as their coffee cups banged; the cooks made noise from the kitchen, and the cutlery of hungry men clanked against the durable stoneware plates to obliterate her desperate cries.

Kristin felt as if she was going to pass out when she neared the dining hall, gasping for breath as she raced down the deserted sidewalks and across the empty parking lot.

"Fire!" she tried to scream, but it came out a rusty croak instead.

She looked toward the building and realized just how fast she had run when she saw the flames just beginning to lick at the structure that housed the children, with tongues of fire intent on consumption.

She lunged for the door of the dining hall just as ranch hands prepared to troop out. The force of impact against the door almost knocked her over.

"Good news, Boss! She's back!"

They gasped, and everyone started to talk at once and barrage her with questions, as they saw her, disheveled, exhausted, almost unable to make sounds as she wildly pointed, trying to signal to them that *she* was all right, but there were children who were not!

"Fire!" she hoarsely croaked.

They looked at each other with uncomprehending amazement, not understanding what she meant. Then the breeze fanned dark smoke toward them as it rolled along on the wind, low to the ground, thick, menacing.

"Oh dear Lord! Smoke! There's a fire!"

"The children—!" Kristin gasped.

Dace rushed past her as if she wasn't even there, yelling over his shoulder for the cook to call the fire department and get pumpers dispatched to the ranch right away.

The cowboys spread like scurrying ants, running toward the extinguishers that had been strategically placed around the ranch while others bolted toward the cabins, praying under their breaths. They fumbled for master keys to let them into the children's rooms so that they could wake the youngsters and prod them toward the door and safety, or carry out those who were too groggy to walk.

Women from the ranch staff came running, and they marshalled the children into a stunned group, watching over them.

"Everything's going to be all right," a motherly worker assured and hugged the children nearest her close to her comforting form.

Kristin joined the women, trying to help calm the children, most who were shivering from the tension of the horrifying sight of the building shooting flames high into the sky as thick, oily black smoke plumed into the air.

"Don't worry about your clothes, honey," a worker assured a blubbering child. "Why, Mr. Kendrick has insurance so that your Mommy will be able to go to the store and buy you beautiful outfits. Nicer than the ones you've been wearing. Brand, spanking new!"

"Sure," another added. "We'll be measuring you children, taking you to town, and buying you shoes before the day is out. We can replace everything. Anything you've lost, we'll get something like it for you."

"But no one can make me another Pooh Bear like Grannie made me," a little girl whimpered. "No one. 'Cause it wasn't store bought. Grannie told me that it was the only one in the whole world like it. She said that I was the only one in the world exactly like me, and my Pooh Bear was that way, too."

"Well, sweetheart, I'll bet that your grannie knows just how much you loved that Pooh Bear, and she'll get out her knitting needles, scissors, fabric, stuffing, and whatever she used, and she'll make you another Pooh just like the one you had."

"She can't," the little girl said, and then began to sob as she realized the full impact of what was happening. "'C. . .cause

Grannie's dead. And now Po. . .Pooh's going to die if I don't save him—"

It took the jolted adults a moment to understand what the child meant, and before they could react, the small child had slipped from the group and begun running toward the room she had just vacated.

"No!" Kristin cried, sprinting after the little girl. "You can't go in there! You can't!"

The child, surely no more than seven years old and scrawny because she'd been so sick, stood in front of the flaming row of once lovely rooms that now where going up in flames, unit after unit.

"Stop!" Kristin ordered as the little girl hesitated.

Kristin thought that she was obeying, but then she realized that her momentary pause had resulted only because she was confused and she wasn't certain which room was hers, as the doors had been left open and there were no helpful numbers to guide her.

Then apparently recognizing something inside the room that was fast becoming illuminated by flames, she darted through the open doorway as the windows gaped blankly, like the vacant eyes in a skull.

Kristin rushed into the unit, trying to grasp the child as she rummaged through the plunder created by the children since the housekeeping staff had cleaned the room the day before. She desperately searched for Pooh.

"Where's Pooh?!" she cried. *"Pooh! Where are you?"*

The child's face was glowing from the flames, drenched in quick sweat from the heat. Fire had crawled up the wallpaper, and was encircling the door. Heat radiated from the ceiling, and Kristin realized that at any instant the roof could come crashing in, burying them beneath a flaming pyre.

The draft created by the inferno was so hot that each breath was agonizing, and Kristin's eyes involuntarily closed against the scorching heat. She felt her hair catch on fire, saw the sparkling effect as the child's hair singed, too, making the child shriek and dance about in hysterical fright.

"Come here!" Kristin cried.

The child, suddenly paralyzed with fear, thinking she was in trouble, about to get a spanking for disobeying an adult, evaded Kristin.

Kristin was crying from pain, shock, and frustration. She dove toward the child, grasped her, and the little girl's nightgown tore, almost freeing her, but Kristin wadded the material around her hands, pulled the little girl toward her, then stumbled toward the only faint opening she could see in what had become a wall of brilliant orange, almost blindingly bright flames.

Kristin's legs felt as if they could no longer move as the heat seared up through the heavy soles of her boots. She heard a rumbling sound, knew that it was the harbinger of tragedy, as the nails and bolts holding the rafters groaned and threatened to pull loose, allowing the roof to crash down as support was destroyed by the fire's devastating force.

"Oh, God." she cried. She thought of the little girl's parents, she thought of Dace's grief, the fact that the child had a life to live, perhaps a man whom she'd grow up and one day love as Kristin knew she cared in that special way for Dace. "Please, Lord, no! Oh. . .give me the strength I need."

From somewhere deep within she found the will to plunge toward the wall of flame in front of her, as she was surrounded by fire on all four sides.

Then there appeared a dark staggering form, silhoutted in the flames as a man bolted ahead, not allowing himself to be driven back by the fire that had become out of control.

Kristin heard mechanical noises, engines whining, and she realized that the pumpers from town were there. There were hissing noises, steam arose, engulfing them, as the firefighters created a wall of water in hopes that it would allow them to walk through the flames alive.

She took a step toward the man—Dace?—surely Dace.

Arms reached out to her. So close, but still seeming so far, far away.

And just when she felt that she should surely die, she clung to the child intent on protecting her, even in their last moments, as the little girl tenaciously hugged her neck, burying her face against the hollow of Kristin's throat the way she'd someday dreamed her own child would.

Kristin felt her oxygen-starved body start to waver, topple, and she was caught in strong arms and pulled toward safety where suddenly all became dark, wet, and she felt herself buffeted mercilessly by the force of the water that made the skin that moments before had blistered with heat grow so cool that she began shivering.

"Get blankets! Keep her warm. An ambulance is on the way. Don't let her slide into shock from the trauma."

As they wrapped her tightly in the blanket, Kristin tried to protest as the searing heat returned to her skin.

Someone tenderly dabbed her face.

And the touch was cool. . .so blessedly cool.

A moment later she heard the child's cry, knew that she was safe. And then Kristin heard no more.

Kristin didn't know how much time had passed before she flickered her eyes open when a cool compress was pressed to her cheeks. Then she felt the searing pain.

"Looks like it's time for another hypo," a crisp, efficient voice said.

"Where am I?" she whispered through lips that felt so dry and parched.

"You're in the hospital—"

Kristin strained to get up, but the nurse's hands eased her back down.

"You're all right. Everyone's fine. The little girl is okay.

She's in better shape than you are, Miss Allen," she murmured.

"Thank God," Kristin said, and began to cry with relief.

"Go ahead and cry. It'll maybe make you feel better," the nurse said. "You've been through a real ordeal. Dace told me what you did—"

"Dace!" Kristin gasped.

"He's been waiting, impatiently, to see you. Do you feel up to receiving company?"

Kristin's hands touched her cheek, her hair, and she felt a sinking sensation. She'd detected blisters. And a charred odor clung to her. "I must look a sight."

"I'm sure you've looked better," the nurse said. "But I know that seeing you alive is the most beautiful sight Dace Kendrick has ever seen. He's got a few blisters himself to mar those handsome features. . . ."

"Show him in," Kristin said, knowing that at last the moment had come.

A moment later, his towering presence seemed to fill the doorway. He slid off his hat and came into the room, his attitude almost reverent.

"Hello, Dace," she whispered as he stepped to her side.

"Kristin, oh Kris. How can I ever make it up to you for being such a fool?"

She remembered Billy Joe's advice out on the lonesome prairie, as she'd been hidden a mere pace or two away, as the man she loved admitted his mistakes.

"You can start by saying, 'I'm sorry,'" she suggested.

"I am sorry," he whispered, seating himself on the edge of the bed, taking her left hand in his. "More sorry than you'll ever know. But somehow saying that I'm sorry doesn't seem like enough."

"It's not," Kristin said. "I have an even better idea. You might try saying, 'I love you.'"

"I have a disturbing sense of *deja vu*."

"We were close then, Dace, although we were never so far apart, it would seem. I heard what you said, what Billy did."

He gave a relieved smile. "Then you know I'm serious about getting to the root of my anger. I do love you, you know. You have the capacity to irritate me, and inspire me, like no other woman I've ever met."

"Not even Janice?" Kristin asked, helpless to contain the question, even as she hated to raise her name at a moment like this.

"Who's Janice?" Dace said. "It seems that nowadays when I look at you, Kristin, I don't see Janice, or her look-alike. I see only Kristin Allen. . .the woman I love and want more than any other gal I've ever known."

"Oh Dace. . . ," Kristin sighed as tears of happiness came to her eyes. "I love you, too. I love you so very, very much."

"Enough to marry me?" he murmured.

Wordlessly Kristin nodded. From the pocket of his jeans he produced the Kendrick family ring, an heirloom handed down to the eldest son, to give his beloved bride.

"Yes. Oh my, *yes!*" Kristin breathed the happy agreement as he slipped the ring on the finger of her left hand that was closest to her heart.

"It's a perfect fit," he observed.

She squeezed his hand. "We're going to be a perfect fit. Forever and ever."

"When are we going to get married?" he asked.

"That's up to you, darling," she said.

"If I had my way, we'd elope on this very day. But the doctor says you've got to remain in the hospital overnight."

"And you're such an impatient man," she clucked in sympathy.

"But so willing to wait for the woman I love, because I know that now we have a fresh beginning. We'll arrange to be married soon enough."

"Ummmm. . .there's always tomorrow. . . ," Kristin reminded.

# *A Letter To Our Readers*

Dear Reader:

In order that we might better contribute to your reading enjoyment, we would appreciate your taking a few minutes to respond to the following questions. When completed, please return to the following:

Rebecca Germany, Editor
Heartsong Presents
P.O. Box 719
Uhrichsville, Ohio 44683

1. Did you enjoy reading *There's Always Tomorrow*?
   ❏ Very much. I would like to see more books
      by this author!
   ❏ Moderately
      I would have enjoyed it more if _____

   _____

2. Are you a member of *Heartsong Presents*?   Yes   No
   If no, where did you purchase this book? _____

   _____

3. What influenced your decision to purchase this
   book? (Check those that apply.)

   ❏ Cover          ❏ Back cover copy

   ❏ Title          ❏ Friends

   ❏ Publicity      ❏ Other _____

4. On a scale from 1 (poor) to 10 (superior), please rate the following elements.

___Heroine    ___Plot

___Hero    ___Inspirational theme

___Setting    ___Secondary characters

5. What settings would you like to see covered in *Heartsong Presents* books?

_____

_____

6. What are some inspirational themes you would like to see treated in future books?_____

_____

_____

7. Would you be interested in reading other *Heartsong Presents* titles?     ❑ Yes     ❑ No

8. Please check your age range:
❑ Under 18     ❑ 18-24     ❑ 25-34
❑ 35-45     ❑ 46-55     ❑ Over 55

9. How many hours per week do you read? _____

Name _____

Occupation _____

Address _____

City _____ State _____ Zip _____

# Norma Jean Lutz

____**Fields of Sweet Content**—When Alecia is summoned to Oklahoma by her sister, she never expected to be in the classroom again, as well as, become the key to unlock the prison of sorrow surrounding a father and his daughter. HP41 $2.95.

____**Love's Silken Melody**—Roshelle Ramone is a star, yet deep, hidden memories and feelings of guilt continue to haunt and paralyze her. Even Victor Moran, the handsome recording company owner, who truly loves her, cannot reach past the darkness of Rochelle's past. HP57 $2.95.

____**Cater to a Whim**—God promised to bless Bandy in all her endeavors, didn't he? Just when things seem to be turning around for Bandy, they fall apart again. An underhanded employee tries to sabotage her business and the new man in Bandy's life seems to be working with her enemies. HP90 $2.95.

\* Watch for **A Winning Heart** (HP121) coming soon from Heartsong Presents.

# ...Hearts ♥ng...

# ..... Presents .....

## Great Inspirational Romance at a Great Price!

*Heartsong Presents* books are inspirational romances in contemporary and historical settings, designed to give you an enjoyable, spirit-lifting reading experience. You can choose from 124 wonderfully written titles from some of today's best authors like Colleen L. Reece, Brenda Bancroft, Janelle Jamison, and many others.

*When ordering quantities less than twelve, above titles are $2.95 each.*

SEND TO: Heartsong Presents Reader's Service
P.O. Box 719, Uhrichsville, Ohio 44683

Please send me the items checked above. I am enclosing $ _____
(please add $1.00 to cover postage per order. OH add 6.25% tax. NJ add 6%.). Send check or money order, no cash or C.O.D.s, please.
**To place a credit card order, call 1-800-847-8270.**

NAME _____

ADDRESS _____

CITY/STATE_____ ZIP _____

HPS MAY

# Heartsong Presents
# Love Stories Are Rated G!

That's for godly, gratifying, and of course, great! If you love a thrilling love story, but don't appreciate the sordidness of popular paperback romances, **Heartsong Presents** is for you. In fact, **Heartsong Presents** is the *only inspirational romance book club*, the only one featuring love stories where Christian faith is the primary ingredient in a marriage relationship.

Sign up today to receive your first set of four, never before published Christian romances. Send no money now; you will receive a bill with the first shipment. You may cancel at any time without obligation, and if you aren't completely satisfied with any selection, you may return the books for an immediate refund!

Imagine. . .four new romances every month—two historical, two contemporary—with men and women like you who long to meet the one God has chosen as the love of their lives. . .all for the low price of $9.97 postpaid.

*To join, simply complete the coupon below and mail to the address provided.* **Heartsong Presents** romances are rated G for another reason: They'll arrive *Godspeed!*